It was extraordinary, she thought, watching him scrape dishes, load the dishwasher.

Yesterday he had seemed as distant as the stars. This evening she was totally at ease with him. Far from being the cold, arrogant prince that his photos suggested, he was intelligent, stimulating, amusing.

"You're not making a bad job of that," she said.

"For a man?"

"For a prince. I don't imagine you've done it before."

"No, but it is simply a question of applying logic and order to the task."

She exploded into a fit of giggles as he closed the dishwasher door, looked at the settings, chose one that seemed appropriate and then switched it on.

"I'm afraid the champagne has gone to your head," he said.

"No, honestly." It was the fact that he hadn't put any detergent in the machine that was so funny.

Welcome to

The lives and loves of the royal, rich and famous!

We're inviting you to the most thrilling
and exclusive weddings of the year!

Meet women who have always wanted
the perfect wedding...but never dreamed
that they might be walking up the aisle
with a millionaire, an aristocrat, or even a prince!

But whether they were born into it,
are faking it or are just plain lucky—
these women are about to be whisked off around the
world to the playground of princes and playboys!

Are their dreams about to come true? If so,
they might just find that they are truly fit for a prince....

Look out for more *HIGH SOCIETY BRIDES*,
coming soon in Harlequin Romance®.

THE ORDINARY PRINCESS

Liz Fielding

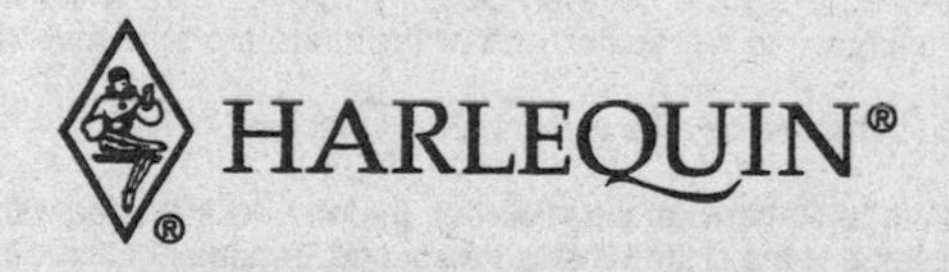

TORONTO • NEW YORK • LONDON
AMSTERDAM • PARIS • SYDNEY • HAMBURG
STOCKHOLM • ATHENS • TOKYO • MILAN • MADRID
PRAGUE • WARSAW • BUDAPEST • AUCKLAND

ISBN 0-373-03773-2

THE ORDINARY PRINCESS

First North American Publication 2003.

This edition published by arrangement with Harlequin Books S.A.

Visit us at www.eHarlequin.com

Printed in U.S.A.

CHAPTER ONE

'FIRED? What do you mean, you've been fired?'

'Sacked, dismissed, given the heave-ho. Released to explore alternative employment opportunities.'

Again.

'I know what the word means, Laura. I was querying the reason.'

'The usual reason, Jay. I have this total inability to concentrate on the task assigned. I'm too easily distracted. In short, my former employer decided that I was more of a liability than an asset.' And with that Laura Varndell picked up her glass of wine and raised it in an ironical toast. 'Here's to the end of my career which today ran into reality and sank without a trace.' And she emptied the glass.

It seemed an appropriate moment to fling it dramatically into the fireplace to underline the end of all her dreams, but since her great-aunt's flat lacked this useful amenity, and flinging it at a radiator didn't quite have the same appeal, she held it out for a refill instead.

Her great-aunt Jenny—known universally as Jay—obliged and, understanding the need for food at such moments, pushed a comfortingly large dish of pistachio nuts in her direction.

It said much for Laura's state of mind that she wasn't tempted.

'All right, let's have it. What did you do this time?'

Jay said this with the unspoken suggestion that, having gone out on a limb, used her contacts—more than once—to get her young niece's stumbling feet on the path to her chosen career, she was not particularly amused that she'd messed up.

'Nothing,' Laura said. That, of course, was why she'd been directed to the exit by her boss. 'Well, when I say nothing that's not strictly true. I did do *something*.'

'Just not what you were told to do, hmm?'

'Just what anyone with an ounce of humanity would have done in my place,' she replied, stung by the unspoken criticism.

'I see.' This said with a convince-me sigh. 'Why don't you start at the beginning.' Jay refilled her own glass as if anticipating the need for fortification.

'I was despatched to cover a demonstration by a senior citizens' action group. The news editor—'

'Trevor McCarthy? I knew him when he couldn't spell the word ''editor'',' Jay said.

Laura had a momentary and deeply pleasing mental image of her fierce news editor as a junior reporter being chewed out by her great-aunt the way he'd chewed her out today. Before directing her to the exit. Then, 'Yes, well, Trevor said that even I couldn't get into trouble with a bunch of OAPs.'

'In other words he's still stupid. You attract trouble like a magnet. One day it'll get you the kind of story that will go around the world.'

'Not if I haven't got a job.' Then, 'To be fair to the man—' although why she should since he'd sacked her, she didn't know '—it should have been simple enough.'

'It's simple enough,' he'd said. *'Even a child could do it.'* Implying that was about her level of competence.

'My brief was to get some quotable quotes, take a few pictures of the oldies in revolt—his words, not mine,' she said quickly, as her own favourite 'oldie' gave her a sharp glance.

'But?'

'I wasn't looking for trouble,' she said, anxious to make that point at the outset. 'I was talking to this really sweet couple, asking them why they were out on a demo when they could have been at home with their feet up in front of the telly, a cup of tea and a toasted bun within easy reach—'

'Being patronising must be catching. Did they hit you with their placard?' Jay enquired dryly.

'No! We were getting along really well, talking about the stupid preconceptions people have about the old. You're the one who's always banging on about the fact that you don't hand over your ability to reason in return for your pension book.' She grinned. 'When you're not back-packing through a snake-infested jungle or canoeing down some gorge or other.'

'But?' her aunt persisted, refusing to be side-tracked.

'But then the old chap sort of keeled over. Collapsed at my feet. I couldn't just ignore that, could I?'

Her aunt's expression suggested that she was withholding judgement pending explanations. 'What caused the collapse?'

'Well, his wife was convinced—*I* was convinced—that it was a heart-attack.'

'But it wasn't.'

'The doctor—and it was hours before he saw a doctor—suggested that it might have been over-excitement. But we didn't know that and I couldn't leave them in the middle of the street, could I?'

Her aunt's face clouded. As a photojournalist she'd covered many war zones and undoubtedly been faced with such dilemmas on a regular basis. But she'd been a professional. Had never forgotten why she was there. She'd always got her story.

'I imagine,' she said, after the slightest of pauses, 'that at this point in the narrative McCarthy asked why you didn't just call an ambulance, summon assistance from a marshal and find someone else to interview?'

'When you put it like that it sounds so simple.'

'It is simple. But I guess you had to be there, hmm?'

'It was all a bit of a muddle, to be honest, and the queue in A&E was horrendous. There'd been an accident on a building site. A wall had collapsed—'

The newsdesk had been trying to contact her about that. They'd wanted her to leave the protest march and cover the building site story, but of course she'd had to switch off her mobile phone in the hospital. She should have phoned in, told them what was happening, but she'd been too intent on staying with the story she had.

'The old lady was so frightened. I couldn't just leave her there. You do understand, don't you?'

'Yes,' she said. 'I understand.' Her tone suggested

that she understood that her great-niece was an idiot. But a sweet idiot.

'By the time he'd been seen by a doctor and I'd got back to the demo I'd missed a mini-riot and thirty-two senior citizens being arrested for committing a breach of the peace.'

'But you did have a human interest story about an old man who'd collapsed from over-excitement,' Jay pointed out.

'Well...' She shrugged, helplessly. 'No, actually.'

'No? You didn't get some heart-wrenching tale of hardship from this pair? In return for all your help?'

Laura shrugged awkwardly. 'Apparently their son is something big in the City. He would have been absolutely furious with them if they'd got their names in the paper.'

'You mean he's a pompous ass who's embarrassed by the fact that his parents have minds of their own?'

'Well, maybe, but you can see his point.' She faltered beneath her aunt's uncompromising gaze. 'Maybe not.'

'You are too kind for your own good, Laura.' Then, because there was no answer to that, she asked, 'What will you do now?'

Laura sighed. 'I don't know. According to Trevor, I ought to forget journalism as a career. Maybe he's right. I haven't exactly covered myself with glory. Apparently a bleeding heart liberal like myself should stick to something more suited to my temperament.' She winced as she remembered his withering scorn. 'In fact he suggested I look for full-time employment as a nanny.'

'In other words he hasn't forgotten the incident with that woman who left you holding her baby.'

Laura closed her eyes and banged her forehead on her knees. 'I'm utterly useless. I'll never make a journalist.'

Jay looked as if she might be about to say something—but thought better of it. 'You're just young, that's all. And a bit soft.'

'They weren't amongst the adjectives Trevor used when he told me to get out and never darken his door again unless I had something he could put on his front page without turning his newspaper into a laughing stock.'

'He said that, did he?' Jay leaned forward and topped up her glass. 'That doesn't sound like the sack to me.'

'No, I got the subtext. My great-aunt is a personal friend of the newspaper's owner so he's covering his back. But, let's face it, he's safe enough.'

'All you need is the right story.'

'I refer to the answer I gave earlier.'

'Hey—' Jay leaned forward, touched her chin, forced her to look up '—whatever happened to your ambition to become a great crusading journalist?'

It had been her ambition for as long as she could remember to emulate her great-aunt, see her byline on stories that moved the world. 'Like you? It's time for a reality check, Jay. I'm not going to make much of a difference if I get side-tracked by sweet old things who need their hands held. I should have been there today, reporting the anger of people who are sick of not being listened to. I should have been at that building site, asking questions about safety. Making sure people know what's going on around them. I should—'

'If you realise that, your day hasn't been entirely wasted. Unless, of course, you plan to just give up and sit there feeling sorry for yourself?'

Laura shrugged, found a smile from somewhere. 'Just give me a minute, okay? I'll get over it.'

'What you need, my girl, is a good old-fashioned scoop. The inside story on someone famous should do it.'

'Oh, that'll be easy.'

'I didn't say it would be easy. I was the one who tried to persuade you that you should forget journalism and look for a sensible job.'

Laura pulled a face. 'My father was a mountaineer, my mother a travel writer, and you spent a fair amount of your time in the world's trouble spots. The family genes would appear to have a sensible deficit.'

Her aunt reached out, touched her arm briefly. Laura blinked, pasted on a smile.

'Even so, I'll pass on an exposé of someone rich and famous, if you don't mind. It isn't my thing.'

'You aren't in a position to be choosy, Laura. The important thing right now is to get you back in favour with the boss. If you really do want to be a journalist?'

Again Laura sensed the unspoken suggestion that this might be the time to call it a day and give 'sensible' a try.

'Of course I do!' She just didn't like some of the stuff journalists did. But Jay was right. She wasn't in a position to be choosy, not if she wanted her job back. 'An exposé?' She pulled a face. 'It would have to be someone totally unsympathetic. Someone I won't go all gooey and protective over.'

'That would help,' Jay agreed, with a wry smile. Then, seriously, 'Someone powerful. Someone who never gives interviews.' And she picked up the gossip magazine she'd been reading when Laura arrived and offered it to her. 'Someone like this.'

Laura glanced at the cover photograph of a man in evening dress—a dark blue ribbon bearing an impressive decoration bisecting his imposing figure—arriving at some glittering state occasion, and then looked again.

'Who is he?'

'His Serene Highness Prince Alexander Michael George Orsino. Crown Prince of Montorino.'

In his early to mid-thirties, the Prince had thick dark hair that no amount of cutting could quite keep from a natural inclination to curl and eyebrows that gave him a look of the devil. He was tall—he stood inches above his companions anyway—and dark. But forget handsome. A smile might have helped, but nothing would ever compensate for a nose that centuries of breeding had perfected for looking down, or the haughty arrogance of his bearing which instantly curdled her natural milk of human kindness.

'Montorino? Isn't that one of those fabulously rich autocratic European principalities?' There had been a recent travel feature in one of the weekend supplements. 'Mountains, lakes, stunning scenery, picturesque medieval buildings?'

'That's the place. And he's the autocrat who'll one day rule it. Nothing to bring out your sympathies there.'

'No,' she said. What she was feeling certainly wasn't sympathy.

He was walking a red carpet laid in his honour with an assurance born of the knowledge that he would rule, as his grandfather now ruled, as his forebears had ruled for a thousand years before him. Absolutely.

As she stared at the photograph his dark eyes seemed to look right at her, challenge her, defy her to do her worst, and a prickle of disquiet, apprehension almost, flickered down her spine. She tossed the magazine away.

'This is all pie-in-the-sky, Jay. I'd never get an interview with a man like him.'

Thank goodness.

'No?' she replied, all innocence. 'Well, maybe Trevor's right. Journalism is an overcrowded profession, after all. And a good nanny can earn a fortune.'

'Excellency.'

'What is it, Karl?'

'I do not wish to alarm you, sir, but Her Royal Highness does not appear to be in the residence.'

'Then your wish is granted, Karl. I am not alarmed. Her Royal Highness is sulking because I refused permission for her to go to a club this evening with some girls from school. She is no doubt hiding in an attempt to frighten us all. The sooner everyone stops panicking and gets about their business, the sooner she'll reappear,' he said dismissively, returning to the papers demanding his attention.

But his concentration had been disturbed. While it was true to say that he was not alarmed, he was concerned. At seventeen, Katerina was too young to marry, or go to clubs. But she was too grown up to send to bed with a scolding. In short she was just the right age to be nothing but trouble.

He sympathised. He'd been seventeen once, long ago. But he had accepted his responsibilities, no matter how unsought, how unwelcome, and applied himself to his duties. If she didn't learn to accept hers, he would have no choice but to send her away from the temptations of London, return her to Montorino until she learned how a royal princess was expected to conduct herself. Something her mother had signally failed to do, but he lived in hope. As he'd hoped to give her this brief time of relative freedom. But if she wouldn't behave...

Karl coughed discreetly, long enough in service to risk ignoring his Prince's impatient dismissal.

'We've searched from basement to attic, sir. Princess Katerina is nowhere to be found.'

'That's because she doesn't want to be found, Karl,' he said. The house was a warren, especially up in the attics. A clever teenager with a serious attack of the sulks could hide up there for a week if she felt so inclined. He had far more important matters to deal with than a girl set on irritating her elders. 'She wouldn't have been foolish enough to leave the building without her security officer.' He caught Karl's doubtful expression. 'And even if she was, she couldn't have got out without someone seeing her. Could she?'

There was only the merest suggestion of hesitation before the man replied, 'No, sir.'

* * *

Laura had woken early from a disturbed sleep with Prince Alexander's face imprinted on her brain. His dark eyes arrogantly challenging her to take him on if she dared.

She'd ignored it.

She had much better things to do than waste her time on someone who looked down his nose at the world from his lofty serenity. Since going to work wasn't one of them, she pulled on her sweats and went for a run.

After that she took a shower, made coffee, ate the croissant she'd picked up at the bakery on the corner and scanned the newspapers in search of a job. There weren't any.

At least nothing that she wanted to do. But then she'd set her heart on journalism and anything else would be failure.

She propped herself up on her elbows. Jay was right. She needed a story—something big enough to persuade Trevor that she wasn't a waste of space. A follow-up on that building site story, perhaps. She booted up her laptop and logged on to the internet to do some in-depth research on the company involved.

But His Serene Highness's image would keep intruding, as fresh as the photograph on the cover of that magazine. As challenging. Refusing to go away.

It was her aunt's fault, of course. Insisting that she take the magazine away with her. She retrieved it from beneath her bed and carried it through to the kitchen. She'd gone to sleep drooling over the frocks at the latest show-biz wedding, studiously avoiding the colour spread of the glittering gala in aid of some charity of which he was the patron. In the light of day, she told herself, he would look a lot less dangerous.

She poured a fresh cup of coffee and stared at the photograph on the cover. He stared right back, as dangerous as ever. And the longer she looked at his implacable features, the more she wanted to disturb that aristocratic bearing. Ruffle that calm poise. Unsettle him as much as he was unsettling her.

So what was stopping her?

Her date with a cowboy builder, that was what. A real story. The internet had provided very little background; she'd have to use the newspaper library. It might be a waste of time, but it was an excuse to put job-hunting on hold.

Except that once she was in the library her mind would keep wandering back to Prince Alexander. She finally abandoned the builder and keyed Montorino into the search engine.

It didn't help much.

While his family had provided hot gossip for the newspapers for most of the previous century, and for a while Prince Alexander had looked set to follow their example, these days he was the very model of what a modern prince should be. Diligent. Hard-working.

Boring.

Well, that was good, wasn't it? For the people of Montorino and for her. Now she could concentrate on something important, right?

Wrong.

Boring?

She wasn't buying that. That face didn't belong to a bore.

She continued her searches and by the end of the day she had an impressive dossier containing the official version of the history of Montorino, the entire Orsino family tree going back to the Middle Ages and enough photographs to fill the family album.

One, of Alexander as a small boy holding his grandfather's hand, looking desolate at his parents' funeral, leapt off the page to touch her heart. She swallowed. Made a quick note that his mother and father had died in a boating accident when he was six, at which point Alexander had become heir to the throne, bypassing his aunts and his older sister since women were barred from the top job in Montorino.

They could have appealed to the Court of Human Rights—in Laura's opinion it was their duty—but they were clearly having too much fun filling the gossip columns of Europe.

Not Alexander. The only photographs of him in the last eight years were formal, controlled images that gave nothing away. Or else they'd been taken at grand occasions where everyone was on their best behaviour, which was much the same thing.

The articles about him were no better. They read like handouts from his public relations department. This bachelor prince, who had effectively become head of state since his grandfather's heart bypass, apparently did nothing but open hospitals, support charities and promote his country. Of course, when he said 'his' country, that was exactly what he meant.

It wasn't just the architecture that was medieval. Which, along with the lack of equal opportunities for princesses, was a situation absolutely guaranteed to raise Laura's democratic hackles.

Jay had been right about one thing. His disturbing eyes notwithstanding, this was a man who would never win her sympathy.

Which was great. As far as it went. She'd have no problem in exposing his Achilles' heel—always assuming he had one—and she'd positively enjoy giving him a wake-up call for the twenty-first century.

It was practically her *duty*, for heaven's sake.

Unfortunately, she had no idea how she was going to go about it. When she'd said that she'd never get an interview with a man like that, she hadn't even been close. It would have made no difference if she'd been one of those rarefied journalists who regularly interviewed the crowned heads of Europe.

His Highness didn't give interviews.

And there was no gossip. Not recent gossip. He might be a bachelor but he wasn't a playboy. It had been years since he'd frequented casinos, squired supermodels to nightclubs, got into brawls with the paparazzi.

All that had ended the day his grandfather had had a heart attack and he'd become head of state in all but name.

On the surface, it seemed that there was no story.

Except, of course, there was always a story if you knew where to look for it. He was flesh and blood, after all. He put on his trousers one leg at a time, the same as any other man. He would have hopes, desires, dreams, just like the lowliest of his subjects. And she didn't imagine he lived like a monk.

Those eyes didn't belong to any monk.

The thought made her shiver a little before she pulled herself together and reminded herself that he might as well have been for all the gossip that made print.

As she'd read everything she could find, hitting a blank wall whenever she'd tried to dig beyond the surface, she'd felt a stir of indignation that anyone with such a public presence could keep his personal life so *private*.

Her research, far from satisfying her curiosity, had piqued it. Far from answering her questions, it had simply raised more.

It was a challenge.

What topped the 'want' list of the man who already had everything? What place did love have in his life? For a man so apparently driven by duty it seemed strange that he hadn't done what was expected of him, married some suitably aristocratic woman and secured the succession.

Or hadn't he found anyone to match his own apparent perfection?

It was, in the end, the very lack of any story that irritated her into action. Coupled with the knowledge that whoever broke through the icy façade to expose the real man would be an editorial favourite. All past mistakes forgiven.

It had to be a façade, surely? No one could be that perfect.

She'd messed up a promising career with a series of stupid blunders that had her spiralling down the ladder rather than climbing it, despite the hefty leg-up from her aunt. She had one last chance to redeem herself—she owed it to Jay to redeem herself—and that prickle of disquiet at the way his eyes had looked out of the magazine at her, seeming to taunt her with his invulnerability, suggested that this was the man to provide the story.

Nonsense, of course. He wasn't taunting her. He was invulnerable and he knew it.

Nonsense it might be, but come evening she was standing outside his grand official London residence, staring up at tall, lighted, first-floor windows and wondering what he was doing up there.

Living up to his public relations image and working late into the night on matters of state?

Watching sport on the television, feet up, his supper on a tray after a hard day doing whatever it was that autocratic rulers did?

Best of all—career-wise—would be if he were entertaining, very discreetly, some lovely young woman.

A royal romance was always news. If she broke that story she'd be a media heroine overnight.

Not that a discreet young woman would go through the front door for everyone to see. She'd probably be driven into the mews at the rear, well away from prying eyes.

She crossed the road to check it out, her well-rehearsed 'stray kitten' story ready, just in case she was challenged by a security guard. As she hesitated at the entrance to the cobbled lane, wondering what on earth she thought she was doing, she heard something drop to the ground ahead of her.

A small bag.

She glanced up. Something darker was moving against the lighter stone of the building.

Not something. Someone.

Hardly the prince's light of love, not climbing

down a drainpipe. It had to be a burglar making off with state papers, or jewels. Imagination in overdrive, she took off down the lane without a thought for her own safety and launched herself at the shadowy figure as it jumped lightly to the ground, bringing the miscreant down with a flying rugby tackle.

They hit the cobbles, and Laura's initial intention to yell for help was thwarted by the fact that she was momentarily winded. Besides, the burglar was making enough noise for both of them. Except it immediately became apparent that this wasn't any ordinary burglar. Not if the high-pitched yell of fright was anything to go by.

This burglar was a girl, slight of figure and terribly young. And then, as her face was lit up by passing car headlights, she realised that she wasn't any ordinary girl, either. It was a face she'd seen during her research on Prince Alexander. His niece. His sister's youngest daughter, Princess Katerina Victoria Elizabeth.

'Oh, sugar,' she said.

The young princess, less restrained, was venting her feelings with scatological exactitude. 'I suppose you're Xander's idea of a watchdog?' she demanded, once she'd thoroughly relieved her feelings.

Xander? 'Oh, you mean His Serene Highness. Er, well—'

'He'll give you the Order of Merit for this, I shouldn't wonder. Second class.'

She stowed her curiosity as to the number of classes the Order of Merit boasted and, playing for time, went for stupid. 'Sorry?'

'In gratitude for breaking my ankle.' And she

moaned. 'It's the one guarantee that I won't be doing this again any time soon.'

'You've broken your ankle?'

'No,' she said, and moaned again. Louder. 'You did that. When you flattened me.'

Stupid was right. 'Oh, good grief. I'm so sorry, but I thought you were a burglar,' Laura said, belatedly scrambling to her knees and taking a closer look. Princess Katerina was wearing a pair of serious boots—eighteen-hole jobs. Good support for her injured ankle, but they made an examination of the injury impossible. 'Are you sure it's broken?' she asked, desperately hoping it might just be a bad sprain. 'Which one is it?'

'Does it matter?' the princess demanded. Then, 'It was the right ankle, okay? And of course I'm sure it's broken. I felt it crack.' She tried to sit up and cried out as she fell back.

Laura felt sick. 'Can you get up? You need to get inside as quickly—'

'Of course I can't get up!'

'If I help you up? You could lean on me—'

'Don't you think you've done enough damage? Look, just get some help, will you?'

The story of her life, she thought, pulling out her cellphone. 'I'd better call an ambulance—'

'No!' She lifted her head. 'Go to the house and ask for Karl. Tell him Katie sent you. And don't tell anyone else what's happened.'

Laura stripped off her jacket, folded it and tucked it beneath the girl's head and shoulders. 'I don't like leaving you here on your own.'

'I'll be fine. Trust me. I'm not going anywhere.'

'No. Look, I'm really sorry—' The girl's wince of pain as she lay back on the jacket brought her apologies to a premature end. 'I'm going.'

The princess caught her hand. 'Just bring Karl,' she gasped, her face screwed up with pain. 'No one else. He's known me since I was a baby and I can persuade him to tell my uncle that I fell downstairs.' There was a mute appeal in her eyes. 'I'm not supposed to be out, you see.'

Somehow that didn't come as a surprise. If her outing had been authorised she'd have left by a more orthodox route accompanied by appropriate security. However, since she had no intention of telling His Serene Highness that she'd broken his niece's ankle, she was happy enough to reassure the girl.

'I'll bring him,' she said. Then she grinned. 'But only if you promise me you won't tell anyone what really happened. I don't relish the idea of being sued for assault and battery.'

'It's a deal.' Princess Katerina started to laugh, then caught her breath as the pain cut in. 'Please go.'

She didn't want to leave the Princess, but the mews was quiet. She should be safe enough for a minute or two.

'I'll just be a minute, okay?' The only answer was another groan and Laura turned and ran back down the street to the huge front door. She put her finger on the bell and kept it there until it was opened by a footman.

A footman!

'Yes, miss?' he enquired, looking down his nose in a manner he must have learned from the Prince.

'May I speak to Karl?' she asked politely. And

prayed that he wouldn't ask, Karl who? She should have asked the Princess that. It would help if she knew who, exactly, Karl was. Trevor was right. She would never make a journalist.

'Who shall I say is calling?' he replied.

'It doesn't matter who I am. Just get him, will you? It's really urgent,' she pressed, when the man's appraising look—the kind that took in her general appearance and suggested she was kidding herself if she thought she was ever going to step foot over any threshold for which he was responsible—had gone on for a great deal longer than was polite. Then, crossing her fingers, she added, 'Tell him Katie sent me.' That did the trick. His expression did not change, but he instantly opened the door and stood back to let her inside.

'Come in,' he said, not so much an invitation as an order. Since she wanted nothing more than to step inside the Prince's palatial London residence, she did as she was told. It was just as well she hadn't been congratulating herself on her good fortune. She got no further than the porter's room beside the front door. 'Wait here.'

Not that she could concentrate on her surroundings. She was too worried about the Princess to absorb the finely carved mouldings, the squared black and white marble flooring, the elegant staircase that she glimpsed through the doors to the vast inner reception hall.

Okay, so she'd got that much.

But she was definitely too worried to congratulate herself that it had taken her less than twelve hours to breach the defences of this most private of royals. With a potential ally on the inside.

She'd been waiting less than thirty seconds when the door behind her opened, and she spun round prepared to spill out the disaster to some venerable old family retainer.

Instead she found herself confronted by the devil himself. The owner of the face that had been haunting her for the last twenty-four hours. The reason for her presence on the footpath opposite.

Even without the white tie and tails, the blue silk of an Order ribbon, there could be no doubt that she was in the presence of a man who knew he was born to rule. Even in what, for him, were undoubtedly casual clothes—linen chinos, an open-necked shirt, cashmere sweater—he still had an air of authority that made her wish she hadn't listened to his niece but had gone with her first thought and called an ambulance.

'Where is Princess Katerina?'

Well, she thought, that was royalty for you. Anyone else would have said, 'Where is my niece?' or 'Where is Katie?' But they never forgot that they were different. Never let the mask slip.

Prince Alexander hadn't raised his voice. He didn't need to. He spoke with the natural authority of his rank, leaving her in no doubt that he expected her to answer him swiftly and truthfully or suffer the consequences, and at this point Laura's sympathies were all with the Princess. She could certainly see why she'd hoped to keep her escapade from her uncle. But there was no hope of secrecy now. The footman had done what he'd seen as his duty. And the Princess needed warmth and medical attention.

'She's outside. I'm afraid she's broken her ankle.'

'I see.' That was it. The man was ice. She'd just told him that his niece was lying hurt on the pavement and he responded with a calm that sent a chill whiffling down her spine. 'Show me.'

The footman held the door for them and he indicated, wordlessly, that she should lead the way. It was all she could do to stop herself from backing out as, equally wordlessly, she did as she was bid with a silent apology to Katie. So much for her friend on the inside.

'She's down there, on the left, in the mews,' she said as he followed her into the street.

Except, of course, she wasn't. The cobbled lane was empty. The Princess—and her favourite jacket—had disappeared.

CHAPTER TWO

LAURA came to an abrupt halt. 'She was here,' she said, looking around her in confusion.

The Princess might have realised that she could move after all—tried to make herself more comfortable while she waited—but she wasn't anywhere within a hundred yards. If she could have moved that far, surely she'd have gone home? Even if home meant trouble.

'I left her just here,' she insisted, pointing to the spot where they'd both crashed to the cobbles.

'With a broken ankle?' Prince Alexander did not sound convinced. He glanced up at the nearby drainpipe. 'How far did she fall?' he asked, without waiting for explanations. He evidently knew his niece very well indeed.

'She didn't fall,' she began, then stopped.

She had no wish to dwell on what—or who—had caused the injury. Besides, there were more important things to worry about. Like, what had happened to the Princess? Two minutes ago she'd been lying where they were standing. Injured, unable even to attempt to hobble to the front door. Now she'd vanished into thin air.

'I left her just here,' she said. 'I put my jacket under her head and—'

'It's not here now,' he said, cutting short her explanation.

'I was just going to say that!' Then, 'Oh!' She turned and stared up at the Prince in total horror as the reality of what must have happened sank in. 'She's been kidnapped, hasn't she? And it's all my fault!'

'I doubt that.' Prince Alexander appeared totally unmoved by her dramatic declaration. Or the fate of his niece. Clearly he didn't understand what she was telling him.

'Yes, really!' she insisted. It was no good. She'd have to own up. 'Look, I saw her climbing down the drainpipe and I thought she was a burglar, so I tackled her to the ground.' His dark brows rose imperceptibly. Actually, putting it baldly like that it did seem pretty unlikely, she realised, but after the briefest pause she pressed on with her confession. 'That's when she broke her ankle. As I said, my fault. I didn't want to leave her—'

'But she insisted?' Then, without giving her an opportunity to reply, 'I wasn't actually referring to your culpability, merely to your reasoning.'

What?

'Look, I don't know what you're talking about. Princess Katerina told me that she wasn't supposed to be out. I get the picture, okay? You're mad at her and she's in trouble. But that scarcely matters under the circumstances. She's disappeared and you have to do something. Now!'

'I'm sorry, Miss—' He paused, offering her an opportunity to introduce herself.

'Varndell,' she completed quickly. She was beginning to suspect that this was a man who wouldn't do anything until the social niceties had been satisfied.

No matter what the emergency. 'Laura Varndell. But I really don't think—'

'Alexander Orsino,' he replied, offering his hand. 'How d'you do?'

That was it. Enough.

'This isn't a cocktail party!' she declared furiously, ignoring his hand. 'And I know who you are. All I want to know is what you're going to do about finding your niece!'

'Nothing while I'm standing in this alley-way,' he informed her, his voice cool enough to freeze a whole pitcher of cocktails. 'If you'll come back into the house—?'

Ice? Had she thought the man was made of something as warm as ice?

'I don't want to go back into the house!'

What was she saying!

Hadn't she been standing on the pavement trying to come up with some plan to get herself invited inside? Her whole career depended upon it. Possibly. But right now Princess Katerina's disappearance took precedence.

'I want you to call the police—or Special Branch—or the Diplomatic Protection Squad. Right now!' she demanded, when he didn't leap to her command.

'And how do you suggest I do that?' he enquired, apparently unperturbed by the crisis.

The 'serene' bit of his title wasn't just for show, apparently. But this wasn't a time for serenity. It was a time for panic.

'Shout?' he offered, when she didn't help him out.

The air left her lungs with a little whoosh, deflating along with the rest of her. 'No, sorry—of course not,' she muttered. Then she laughed. Well, it was more of a giggle, really, but even so quite unforgivable under the circumstances. 'I don't appear to be thinking very clearly.' Which had to be the understatement of the year. 'I'm not used to this kind of thing.'

'You've had a shock, Miss Varndell, one for which my niece will, in due course, apologise. In the meantime I really do think you should come inside. Take a moment to recover.'

It was hysterics, of course. The desperate urge to giggle. In some small rational part of her brain she recognised that. This man's niece had been kidnapped and all he was concerned about was that a total stranger might have suffered a little shock.

Noblesse oblige was safe in the hands of His Serene Highness Prince Alexander Michael George Orsino.

And why would she be complaining, exactly?

She'd got her wish. The Prince was inviting her into his home and handing her a scoop on a plate. The inside story on a royal kidnapping was just what she needed to get back into Trevor McCarthy's good books. The very least she could do was to say 'thank you' very nicely and let His Serene Highness take her inside so that she could do her research in comfort.

While she was recovering.

Slowly.

So that she could watch the story unfold around her.

'Thank you,' she said, as nicely—if somewhat breathlessly—as she knew how. 'I do seem to be feeling a little bit shaky.'

One moment it was an act, the next it was nothing but the truth as the Prince took her elbow in his palm and directed her firmly towards his front door. His manner suggested that, thoughtful though his invitation had appeared, he'd had no intention of letting her go anywhere until he'd grilled her about her involvement in his niece's disappearance.

She swallowed.

It would make great copy, she reminded herself.

Once she'd got bail.

He paused as they reached the lights of the elegant porticoed entrance, glancing down at her, his devilish eyebrows drawn down in the slightest frown and, for just a moment, she thought those dark eyes could see right through her. Read her mind.

'You've grazed your cheek, Miss Varndell,' he said. She instinctively lifted her hand to check, but he caught her wrist, stopping her. 'And your knuckles.'

'It's nothing,' she said automatically, her expensive boarding-school having instilled the stern lesson that ladies did not make a fuss.

Fortunately, Alexander Orsino ignored her stoicism.

'I'll get someone to see to them,' he said, every inch the autocrat.

He paused to speak briefly to the footman in a language that wasn't quite Italian, or French, but a Montorinan dialect that her brain wasn't quite up to unscrambling at such speed. It was already fully occupied.

The man bowed in acknowledgement and backed away while Prince Alexander, his hand still welded firmly to her elbow, led her towards a wide curving staircase without another word.

She should be looking around, she thought, as she

attempted to keep a grip on reality. She should be taking mental notes. But she was having trouble enough just catching her breath.

The man was right. She had to be in shock. That would explain why she had the oddest feeling that she'd stepped into the set of an operetta, with its sweeping staircase, crystal chandeliers and very superior footman wearing black tails.

Add to the mix a cold-hearted prince, a peasant girl and a missing princess—there were all the ingredients for a fairy tale frivolity.

The clothes were all wrong, of course. Peasant girls wore dirndl skirts and embroidered blouses—at least in operetta—while she was wearing a pair of extremely functional cargo pants and a sweatshirt of such antiquity that whatever words had originally been splashed across her bosom had long since faded to illegibility.

Not that the Prince, with his open-necked shirt and cashmere sweater, was getting more than three out of ten for effort. Didn't he dress for dinner, for heaven's sake?

Where were his standards?

She dragged herself back from the beckoning arms of hysteria as he opened a door and ushered her into a book-lined room that clearly doubled as sitting room and study.

Here, the baroque evaporated and they were back in the twenty-first century. Computers, a couple of large sofas, a functional desk and enough paperwork to keep an average-sized business going for a month. But running a small country presumably entailed a vast amount of paperwork, and for just a moment she felt a twinge of sympathy for the man. No time to put his feet up with the television, or a pretty girl for this prince.

'Brandy?' he offered.

'What?' Distracted, she turned back to the Prince. 'I think the princess's welfare is more important right now. What are you going to do about finding her?' she asked. But politely. She suspected that she'd already stretched her luck to breaking point.

'Nothing. I know where she is. Please make yourself comfortable, Miss Varndell,' he continued, indicating one of the sofas.

'You know?'

'More accurately, I know where she's going. My niece wished to go to a club with some friends. I refused to give permission. She is, after all, under age.' He shrugged. 'I've despatched her security officer to bring her home.'

She stared at him. 'Are you crazy? Weren't you listening? She had a broken ankle!'

'Are you absolutely sure about that?' he replied as he took her hand and placed an exquisite crystal glass in it, closing his long fingers around hers until he was certain she had it safely. Long, slender fingers, one of them bearing a heavy gold signet ring embossed with his personal coat of arms. 'Did you see it for yourself?'

She blinked, looked up. 'See what?'

'Princess Katerina's ankle?' he prompted.

'Oh. Well, no, she was wearing boots, but she said—'

She'd said it was broken—had groaned convincingly. Laura subsided on to the sofa as she realised that, once again, she'd been played for a fool.

'Oh, I see. You're suggesting that she was just pretending. Playing hurt to get rid of me while she made good her escape.'

'I would say it's more likely than a chance kidnapping, wouldn't you?'

It would certainly explain why she'd insisted on being left where she was rather than attempting, with help, to make it inside, which would have been her own choice under the circumstances, no matter how painful. She took a sip of the brandy, felt the steadying warmth as it slipped down.

She'd been very convincing.

'How can you be so sure?' she asked.

Prince Alexander lifted one eyebrow the merest fraction of a millimetre as he poured another measure for himself.

'Oh, I see. She's done this before.'

'Not Katerina. She wouldn't have managed it twice,' he assured her in a tone that left her in no doubt he was telling the truth.

'So how do you—?' And then, in a flash of intuition, she realised that the Princess was not the first member of the Royal House of Orsino to have made a break for freedom. Prince Alexander might have had something of a reputation as a young man, but he'd only been following a trail blazed by his older sister.

'She not only looks like her mother, but has apparently inherited her *laissez-faire* attitude to personal behaviour,' he admitted stiffly. 'You have my sincerest apologies for the fright you've been given, Miss

Varndell. My niece will make her own apologies in due course.'

Under normal circumstances two Miss Varndells were about as much as she could take before she begged to be called Laura. Outside, on the pavement, she might have begged. Inside, his formality made such a request unthinkable.

'That's not important. I'm just relieved that she's not in danger.' Then, 'This security character—he's not going to haul her out of the club, is he?' She imagined how humiliated she'd feel under such circumstances. 'It'll only make her more resentful,' she began. Then stopped. 'I'm sorry. It's none of my business.'

'No, it isn't.' Then, with the faintest crease softening the corners of his eyes, 'But if you'll forgive me for saying so, it's somewhat sexist of you to assume that her security officer is male.'

A crack in the ice? He was a lot more attractive when he smiled. Almost human.

'Did you really think I'd send some uniformed heavy to barge in and drag her home?' The smile deepened in response to her embarrassed flush. 'There's no need to answer that. I may be a monster—my niece certainly believes so—Miss Varndell, but I was once a *young* monster with my own problem with rules.'

'But you're still going to have her brought home.'

'Certainly.' Then, 'You have some objection?'

'It's not my place to object. I just think that making a public spectacle of the girl isn't likely to improve matters.'

'You're suggesting that with a proper chaperon she should be allowed to stay for a while?'

'A chaperon? Heaven forbid! I'm sure she'd rather come home than submit to that,' she said. Just to see how deep the crack went. 'Poor girl.'

'Scarcely that,' he replied, abruptly losing the smile. Not very far, then.

'There's more than one way to experience poverty,' she muttered, but not quietly enough, and his eyebrows rose with sufficient alacrity to indicate that he was unused to having his actions questioned. Especially since he clearly thought he was being incredibly relaxed about the whole matter.

'You're suggesting emotional impoverishment?' he demanded.

'I wouldn't be that impertinent.'

'Oh, I think you would.'

Cold, but perceptive. He didn't wait for her to admit it, but picked up the telephone and spoke briefly into it before glancing back at her.

She'd been holding her breath, but his expression did not suggest he was about to have her bodily ejected. Yet.

'So,' he continued, as if there had been no interruption. 'Enlighten me. What are you suggesting, Miss Varndell?'

Her mouth dried. Lecturing the man on the best way to raise his niece was not going to get her the prized interview. But it might get her some memorable quotes.

If she provoked him sufficiently she fancied she'd be able to name her price for the story. And Trevor McCarthy would have to stand in line.

'Well?' he demanded.

Well, why not? He'd asked for it, and the least she could do in return for his unwitting assistance in promoting her career was to give the Prince the benefit of her experience.

'Young people need to test themselves against the world so that they can learn from their mistakes. Discover safe boundaries. Keeping them wrapped in cotton wool leaves them vulnerable.' His face remained expressionless. No hint of that smile now. She swallowed nervously. 'Later.'

'You are speaking from personal experience?'

'Well, I'm young,' she hedged. Then realised that the Princess would probably think her well past it at twenty-four. 'Well, youngish,' she amended. 'Young enough to remember being Katie's age.'

Not that she'd had parents to restrict her movements. But school had been worse. You couldn't have a row with an institution. And slamming doors was pointless. You didn't get understanding. You just got a lecture on the subject of thoughtful behaviour, followed by a week of detention.

'Well, thank you for your advice, but I'd rather my niece didn't make her mistakes on my watch. She can return to Montorino to complete her education.'

'That's a little harsh, isn't it? One mistake and she's out?'

His mouth straightened into a hard line that warned her to have a care. Then, presumably because she was an outsider and could not be expected to understand this, he gave a curt bow of the head and, conceding the point, said, 'Maybe it is harsh, but this family has provided the newsprint of Europe with more than enough scandal. I do not want a photograph of Katerina, under age and behaving badly, to appear in your newspapers,' he said.

Her throat dried.

'I suppose the British press is no worse than anywhere else, but they'd make the most of such a story,' he continued.

'Oh, yes. I see.' He'd been speaking generally. It took a moment for her heartbeat to return to something approaching normal. 'It's, um, just as well there wasn't a newspaper photographer lurking outside when she made a break for it, then.'

There was nothing in his expression to suggest that he had even noticed her sarcasm, but his upper lip was so stiff that any kind of expression would have been difficult.

'That kind of photographer only lurks where there is likely to be something worth his time. If tonight's escapade becomes public knowledge they'll be stacked ten deep.'

'It won't become public knowledge, surely? Unless she makes a fuss when the leash is jerked.'

'You're suggesting that if I don't jerk it no one will notice her?'

'Well, she wasn't wearing a tiara.'

'*You* recognised her,' he pointed out.

Oh, sugar. Think. Think. 'Only because she was coming out of your official residence.' Another raised brow queried how she knew that. 'I've seen the flag,' she said, which appeared to satisfy him. 'I wouldn't have recognised her if I'd seen her in the street.'

'No?'

'No,' she said. 'In black denim, and with a hair-do

from hell, she didn't look like anyone's idea of a princess.'

'Nevertheless, seventeen is a dangerous age,' he declared with the confidence of a man who remembered just how dangerous it could be. 'Which is why I am sending her home.'

'It's a dangerous age wherever you live,' she replied. And, since she had nothing to lose, she added, 'Or are the boys in Montorino different? A little less testosterone-driven?' She met his cool stare, matched it, then, with measured insolence, added, 'Sir?'

'Not noticeably,' he admitted after an epic pause. 'But I can be certain that she'll receive appropriate respect there.'

'She's seventeen! She doesn't want respect. She wants to have fun—and you can't keep her locked up in an enchanted tower for ever. Try it and she'll escape with the first good-looking scoundrel with a head for heights—' Too late, she remembered that his sister had done something very like that.

There was a tap on the door and, with the temperature of Prince Alexander's expression sinking in direct proportion to the depth of the hole she was digging with her mouth, Laura seized the opportunity to shut up.

He continued to stare at her for what seemed like for ever before he finally turned away and snapped, 'Come in.'

One of the doors opened and a young maid appeared bearing a first aid box resting on a silver tray. She dropped a curtsey in the direction of the Prince before putting the tray on the table in front of Laura. 'Excuse,' she said, nervously. 'You will—? I will—?'

Laura smiled encouragingly, but the girl was too shy to respond. Instead she picked up the first aid box and, her hands shaking noticeably, tried to open it. The lid at first refused to give but when, in desperation, she gave it a sharp tug it flew open, scattering the contents over the table and floor.

There was a moment of utter stillness before, with a wail of anguish, the girl rushed from the room.

'Why on earth do these silly girls behave as if I'm going to beat them?' the Prince demanded.

'I can't imagine,' Laura said caustically as she bent to retrieve the contents of the box. 'You'd better send her home with Princess Katerina—'

'Leave that!'

She glanced up.

He lifted a hand in a gesture that was at once supplication and exasperation. 'My apologies. I did not mean to bark at you.'

He *was* concerned about Katerina, she realised with a belated flash of insight. Behind that rigid exterior he was just like any man worried about a reckless teenager in his care.

Recalling some of her own wilder moments, she felt her over-developed sense of empathy well up, and another dangerous surge of sympathy for him. She quashed it mercilessly. He did not need her sympathy. Jay had offered him as a target because of his very lack of sympathetic qualities.

'I'm sure she'll be okay,' she said and, ignoring his command, continued to pick up thc dressings.

'Are you?' He bent to help her, folding his long legs as he reached beneath the table. 'It isn't easy.'

'Being her guardian?' she asked, catching her breath as his shoulder brushed against hers.

'Being young,' he countered, concentrating on his task. 'Being so visible. Having every mistake you make the subject of common gossip.'

He was holding a pouch containing an antiseptic wipe as if not quite sure what to do with it.

'Shall I take that?' she offered, holding out her hand.

Alexander Orsino looked up to discover that Laura Varndell was regarding him solemnly, her wide silvery blue eyes apparently brimming over with compassion, concern.

He had no need of her concern. No need of any assistance. He wasn't helpless and to demonstrate the fact, in the absence of the maid, he would deal with her grazes himself.

'Sit down,' he said, tearing open the pouch containing an antiseptic wipe before sitting down beside her. 'Give me your hand.'

For a moment she stared at him in disbelief, then wordlessly—which was probably a first—she did as she was told, holding out her hand for his attention. It was long, finely boned—a hand, wrist, made for the sparkle of diamonds. But it was bare of any kind of adornment other than nail polish.

He supported it, holding it gently as he dabbed at her knuckles with the antiseptic.

She was trembling almost imperceptibly, doubtless still feeling the after effects of her reckless behaviour, and he found himself wanting to tighten his grip, reassure her.

'Tell me, Miss Varndell,' he said, by way of distraction, 'do you make a habit of tackling burglars?'

'I couldn't say. I've never been in that situation before. The truth is, I didn't stop to think.'

'Well, on this occasion I'm glad you didn't,' he said, glancing up and momentarily left struggling for breath as he looked straight into her huge, solemn eyes. 'Will you promise me that next time you think you're witnessing a crime in progress you will walk away? Call the police?'

'If I'd done that today you wouldn't have known that your niece had made a break for freedom,' she pointed out.

'Even so. Promise me.'

'I'll try,' she offered, hooking a strand of pale blonde hair behind her ear to reveal a tiny gold earring in the shape of a star. 'But only if you'll stop calling me Miss Varndell, as if you're addressing a public meeting. I prefer Laura.'

He preferred formality. It was a useful way of keeping his distance. Except, of course, Laura Varndell had already breached his highest defences. Few outsiders ever made it into this room.

Stalling for time, he looked for another antiseptic wipe, took his time about opening it before he turned to face her, lifting her chin with the touch of his fingers, turning her face to the light. She had silver-blue eyes, clear, almost translucent skin that was the gift of cool, northern skies, and stars in her ears. And as she lifted her head, and her flaxen hair slid back from her neck, he found himself imagining how it would look encircled by the wide collar of pearls that had once belonged to his mother.

Which was enough to bring him back to earth.

And, faintly embarrassed to be caught staring, he said, 'It's nothing. No real damage.' But he touched the moist cloth to her cheek to clean away a smear of dust. 'What did you do?'

Her eyes widened. 'Me?'

'You seem very knowledgeable about the dangers of restricting teenage girls. Were you reckless? At seventeen?'

'Oh, I see.' Her lips parted as she laughed. 'I really don't think I should tell you that. I'm on Princess Katerina's side in this and I'd hate to prejudice her case.'

'In other words, yes.' She didn't answer. 'Did you escape down drainpipes?' he persisted. 'Go to clubs and parties your parents had forbidden?'

Her smile faded. 'I had no parents to forbid me. They were killed when I was a child.'

He stilled. 'I'm so sorry, Laura.'

She'd finally touched him with this common bond between them, and for a moment he wanted to say that he understood her loss, her pain—

'It was a long time ago and really I barely knew them,' she said quickly, before he could speak. He recognised the defence mechanism. 'They were always away a lot, and then I was at boarding school, but in answer to your question, yes, Your Highness, I was frequently reckless—although I never climbed down a drainpipe.' Her lovely eyes appeared to cloud momentarily. 'I'm afraid of heights.'

'But not much else, I'd suspect,' he said.

'Then you'd be wrong,' she said, jacking the smile back into place, determinedly shaking off whatever shadow had crossed her thoughts. 'I'm absolutely terrified at this moment.'

He regarded her quizzically. He knew she was a little shaky, had felt the almost imperceptible tremble of her hand as it lay in his, but outwardly she was calm, composed.

'Why?' he demanded. 'You're not like that silly girl, afraid of me.' It was not a question.

'Well, actually I am, just a bit. But only because I know you're going to be angry with me.'

He leaned back, surprised. 'Why would I be angry with you?'

'Because I'm going to ask you to give Katerina another chance. Ground her, if you must,' she rushed on. 'She's been foolish; of course she has. But even princesses need a day off now and then. An opportunity to be ordinary.'

'Ordinary?'

'You know. Girl-in-the-street ordinary.'

'Oh, please.'

'Has she ever been on a bus or the underground?' she demanded. Then, as an afterthought, 'Have you?'

Scarcely sure whether to be amused or affronted, he said, 'I've never found it necessary.'

'The chauffeur is on call twenty-four hours a day, I guess.'

'Not the same one,' he assured her, opting for amusement. He had a feeling it would be safer. 'But, yes. It goes with the job. I am on call twenty-four hours a day, too. Seven days a week. Three hundred and sixty-five days a year.'

'You never have a day off?'

'I escape occasionally.' He put on working clothes,

went to his vineyard to work up an honest sweat. 'But my pager is never switched off.'

'Poor you, too, then,' she responded. And sounded as if she meant it.

'You make it sound as if I am deprived,' he said, suddenly finding even his simulated amusement difficult to sustain. 'I cannot believe, given the choice, that you would surrender a chauffeur-driven car in order to battle with the rush hour crowds on the underground.'

'Maybe not, but you lose something, keeping the outside world at a distance. The underground may be crowded and dirty, but it's real,' she said. 'Using it is a life skill. Like learning to use a public telephone—'

'My niece has a mobile phone,' he said, cutting off her nonsense. 'And I can assure you she knows how to use it. It costs a small fortune—'

'And if she lost it?' she demanded, interrupting him. People did not interrupt him. 'Or it was stolen? This evening, for instance, on her way to this club. If she got into difficulties would she know how to use a public call box?'

Now she was being ridiculous. 'How difficult can it be?'

'Nothing is difficult if you know how to do it. But suppose that first time she was frightened, confused, in a panic? Suppose it was one of those boxes that only takes a pre-paid phone card and she didn't have one?'

Phone card? What was a phone card?

She didn't miss his hesitation and, apparently satisfied that she'd made her point, she said, 'Maybe you should try it for yourself and see.'

'You are not exactly tempting me to allow Katerina more freedom, Laura.'

'Give it to her,' she warned, 'or she'll take it. She nearly got away with it tonight. She'll be a lot safer if she's streetwise. Knows her way around.'

'She will be even safer in Montorino,' he said, getting abruptly to his feet and putting an end to this lecture from a young woman who hadn't the first idea about Katerina's life—or his.

He'd been patient—Laura Varndell had, after all, alerted him to Katie's bolt for freedom—but enough was enough. Then, discovering that he was still holding the wipe, evidence of his sudden and unexpected intimacy with a stranger, he dropped it on the tray as if it was incendiary.

'You've been generous with your time,' he said, 'and your interesting opinions. You have my thanks, Miss Varndell,' he went on, reverting to the safety of formality, 'but I will not delay you any longer. And, despite your enthusiasm for public transport, on this occasion I must insist that you allow my chauffeur to take you home.'

She looked, for just a moment, as if she was about to throw his offer back in his face. Tell him what to do with his lift home.

But she didn't. Instead she gathered herself and stood up. 'Thank you, Your Highness, but that won't be necessary. I have transport.' Her own two feet would carry her to the nearest bus stop. The last thing she wanted was His Serene Highness knowing where she lived. Then, as she reached the door, she turned.

'Will you call me and let me know when Princess Katerina arrives home safely? It doesn't matter how late it is. I won't sleep until I know.'

'Of course.'

'I'll leave my number with the, um, footman, then.'

He resisted the impulse to ask her to leave it with him. He wasn't a secretary. He didn't deal in telephone numbers. 'He will accompany you to your car.'

'There's no need for that. I'm not a princess, Your Highness. I know how to look after myself.'

CHAPTER THREE

LAURA sat at her desk, laptop open. All she had to do was send a little note to Trevor asking if he was interested in an exclusive diary piece involving a spoilt, wayward princess who had so far evaded the attentions of the press. And her encounter with Prince Less-Than-Charming.

He wouldn't be able to resist it.

Short of catching the Prince himself climbing down someone's drainpipe—preferably not his own—it couldn't be more perfect, she told herself. And tried not to listen to the voice of a conscience which would keep repeating Prince Alexander's words about not wanting a photograph of Katerina appearing in some newspaper.

But it wasn't a photograph. She wasn't even going to name names. Not that she supposed there would be any real doubt as to her identity. Katie's days of shinning down drainpipes without being spotted by the paparazzi would be over. But they were anyway.

It would certainly give His Serene Highness ample justification for sending the girl back to Montorino. She was doing him a favour, she rationalised.

If anything, he should be grateful.

She wouldn't hold her breath for his undying thanks. Didn't want them.

All she wanted was a phone call to let her know that the girl was safely back under her uncle's roof, then she could hit 'send' and go to bed safe in the knowledge that Trevor would be calling her tomorrow to offer her her job back.

Xander spoke to the security officer assigned to Katie and, having reassured himself that his niece was safe, gave orders that if she and her friends left the club, went somewhere they wouldn't be actually breaking the law, there was no need for her to return home immediately.

It was nothing to do with Laura Varndell's pleading on her behalf. On the contrary. Katie was, after all, seventeen. She might not be old enough to be in a club, but she was not a child: according to her champion, treating her like one had caused the problem in the first place.

So, having rationalised the likely harm of her staying out for an hour or two against what would happen if she decided to cause a scene, he had chosen the former and returned to what he had been doing before the interruption.

He was finding it unusually difficult to concentrate on state papers, however. Laura Varndell's face—smiling approvingly—would keep intruding. Since her approval mattered not one jot, he did his best to block her out, although farming subsidies faced an uphill battle for his concentration. He persisted, however, until Katie arrived home late, eyes sparkling, apparently unconcerned by the prospect of facing the consequences of her actions.

'I'm sorry, Xander,' she said, twirling dramatically before dropping a kiss on the top of his head, exactly as if he were her great-grandfather. It made him feel about the same age.

'No, you're not, Katerina,' he said, determined upon severity. 'You're not in the least bit sorry.'

'Oh, Lord,' she said, flopping down on a sofa and putting her feet up on the table. 'If it's Katerina, I'm in serious trouble. Am I being sent home on the first available flight tomorrow morning?'

'This morning,' he corrected. 'Right after you've telephoned Miss Varndell to apologise for the fright you gave her when you disappeared.'

'Miss Varndell?'

'The young woman who mistook you for a burglar?'

'I frightened *her*? Give me a break. She practically scared the living daylights out of me.'

'Then, along with your apologies, she has earned my thanks.'

'I'll bet. I told her you'd probably give her the Order of Merit—just second class, you understand, in gratitude for clipping my wings.'

'What a pity she didn't make a better job of it. It would have saved me the trouble.'

'I hope you didn't disappoint her?'

'I gave her my thanks, some first aid and a brandy for the shock. Nothing more.'

'That's so cheap of you.' Then, 'You're not really going to send me home, are you?'

'Goodnight, Katerina.'

'Oh, I see. I have to sweat on it.' She didn't seem unduly bothered as she swung her legs to the floor. 'Goodnight, Your Serene Highness,' she said, dropping him a graceful curtsey—quite a feat considering the hideous boots she was wearing—apparently satisfied that she'd teased him out of his severity.

He watched her go, biting back the smile until she was out of sight. Only then did he pick up the phone.

Laura had *Celebrity* magazine propped up on her desk in front of her as she waited for the call, checking the picture of Prince Alexander against reality. He did have the most incredible eyes. Dark and deep as one of Montorino's mountain lakes. And about as cold.

Except that for a moment as he'd held her face, cleaned the graze on her cheek with such gentleness, she'd almost believed he could be a real human being if he made the effort.

She told herself that she was glad he hadn't bothered. She had an uneasy feeling that, if she cracked the surface, somewhere beneath that austere façade there might be a man it would be all too easy to like and she didn't want to like him.

Her entire future depended upon her not liking him at all.

She turned from the photograph, glaring at the cellphone lying on her desk. 'Ring,' she demanded. 'Just ring, will you!'

She jumped as it responded on cue, the soft burble unexpectedly loud in the late-night silence. That had to be the reason she was shaking as she picked it up, pressed 'receive'. The reason for the warm flush to her cheeks.

She took a deep, steadying breath. 'Laura Varndell.'

'Miss Varndell, His Serene Highness Prince Alexander has asked me to inform you that Her

Highness Princess Katerina has returned home safely.'

The deep breath came in handy because, for just a moment, everything stopped working.

She didn't believe it—it was the *footman*! He'd asked that pompous prat in the tailcoat to call her. So much for her belief in the real human being beneath the cold exterior.

What had she been thinking? He was a prince. Reality didn't come into it.

'Please thank His Serene Highness for his courtesy,' she replied, through gritted teeth. Then she turned to her laptop and the note waiting to be despatched to Trevor McCarthy.

And she hit 'send'.

Xander sat back, ignoring the pile of papers still to be dealt with before he could even think about bed. Regretting that he hadn't called Laura Varndell himself to tell her that Katie was safely home.

He made a dismissive gesture.

That he'd even been tempted was sufficient reason in itself not to call, he knew, yet there had been something about her directness that was deeply appealing. She had an opinion and wasn't afraid to voice it.

He was so tired of people saying only those things they thought he wanted to hear. Of people who agreed with him without question. Of timorous maids who dropped things if he so much as looked at them.

Laura hadn't been afraid of him. Better still, she hadn't been trying to impress him. Given the opportunity, she would undoubtedly tell him that it was his fault if his staff were terrified of him. He eased the back of his neck, kneading his fingers into the knots of tension that had eased for a while, but had now returned with a vengeance.

She just didn't have a clue about his life. Fortunate girl.

Not that it mattered. She would have been worth listening to, no matter what ridiculous ideas she was propounding. Even lobbying for Katie's right to the kind of freedom other girls of her age enjoyed.

As if he took some perverted pleasure in keeping his niece from running wild. The girl was in London to further her education, not to party. There would be a media feeding frenzy soon enough. Eager eyes watching, waiting for her to put a foot wrong.

'Ordinary' girls could get away with breaking the rules. Katie wasn't ordinary, and he wanted her to be mature enough to cope with those pressures before she stepped into the spotlight.

That Laura meant well he did not doubt, but the very idea of 'time out' from being a princess was ridiculous. There was no 'time out'. It was a life sentence—

Enough. He did not have to justify himself to some passing stranger with an over-developed sense of public duty. Even one whose voice had bubbled with laughter, the joy of life. For a moment, sitting close to her, he had felt as if all he had to do was reach out, hold her and he would feel it, too.

Ridiculous.

He picked up the next file from those awaiting his attention.

Katie would call her tomorrow. Make her apologies. Send Laura Varndell some appropriate token.

There was a selection of small pieces of jewellery bearing the Montorino coat of arms kept for exactly this purpose. A brooch, perhaps. He was sure there was a brooch....

'"Milk Quotas".' He read the name on the report in front of him, saying it out loud, forcing his attention back to the matter in hand. Dragging his hand over his face to keep himself awake.

Forget Katie—he was the one in need of a day off.

It wasn't going to happen. He was in London to fly the flag for his country; create interest in Montorino's fledgling tourist industry by appearing at all manner of high society events; sign trade agreements; support the charities of which he was a patron.

All of which had been orchestrated so that he could stay in London to keep an eye on Katie while she spent three months on a student exchange visit.

Some job he was making of that. She'd been here just over a week and already she was getting into trouble. It had only been Laura Varndell's presence of mind that had alerted him to her escapade. He felt a chill ripple through him at the thought of her climbing down that drainpipe. If she'd really fallen—

He gave up on the report, finished the brandy he'd poured earlier. Laura had barely touched hers, he noticed. He frowned, wondering why she was afraid of heights, as he picked up her glass, placed it beside his on the tray before abandoning the problems of agricultural subsidies and heading for bed.

Not a brooch, he decided as he turned out the light. Young women didn't wear brooches. She would just put it in a drawer and forget about it.

Which actually would not be such a bad thing.

He should do the same.

'Laura?'

Laura clamped the phone beneath her chin and groped for the bedside clock, looking at the time before lying back with a silent groan. She'd forgotten to set it and, after another night in which sleep was transient, disturbed by dreams in which cold dark eyes had burned with a repressed heat and tender hands…

Trevor McCarthy's voice cut through her sleepy thoughts, dragging her back to the real world. 'Did I wake you?'

'Trevor—' She laughed to cover a yawn. Ha, ha, ha. 'Of course not. I've been awake for hours.' Which was true. It was only as the birds had begun to twitter that she'd finally fallen into a deep sleep.

'I got your e-mail.'

'Great,' she said. So why wasn't she more thrilled that he hadn't wasted any time in calling her about it?

'So? Surprise me. What have you got?'

She might be short of sleep, but she wasn't stupid. 'Nice try, Trevor, but if I tell you that why would you take me back?'

'No reason at all. I take it we're talking about Princess Katerina?'

That got her full attention and she sat up. 'How do you know that?'

'Bad news. The opposition scooped you. There's a picture in the *Courier* this morning of Her Royal Highness arriving at some club.'

Oh, great! Katerina had chosen to break the rules

at a place with a paparazzi encampment and now her exclusive had been blown right out of the water. It was as if someone was trying to tell her, repeatedly, that she just wasn't meant to be a journalist.

'You should have turned in your story last night, instead of playing hard to get. Now, if there's nothing else, I've got a paper to get out—'

'Of course there's something else,' she rapped out. 'That photograph is nothing compared to what I have.'

'Do you want to share?' he enquired. She wasn't fooled by his bored voice. Royal stories were like gold dust.

'Prince Alexander?' she offered.

'What about him?'

'I spent some time in his inner sanctum last night. Talked to him.' She sensed she had his total attention. 'Are you interested?' she asked.

'That depends on what he said. Any pictures?'

Pictures? Did the stupid man think that Prince Alexander would just sit back while she took snaps for her family album?

'It was a chance encounter, Trevor. I didn't have a concealed camera about my person.'

'No problem. I'll bike one over to you. When can you deliver?'

'When?' she repeated, playing for time. So far out of her depth now that she was treading water.

Rescue came in the form of a long peal on the doorbell. 'Trevor, there's someone at the door,' she said. 'I'll call you back.'

'Don't bother unless you have pictures.' Before she could answer, she was listening to the dialling tone.

She grabbed her wrap as there was a second insistent ring, dragging her fingers through her slept-in hair. Not that it mattered how she looked—it was undoubtedly the guy from the top-floor studio flat, an out-of-work actor who couldn't afford decent coffee so drank hers instead. He wasn't usually so impatient. He must be desperate for caffeine.

It wasn't Sean.

It was Her Highness Princess Katerina Victoria Elizabeth of Montorino.

Last night she had been dressed entirely in wild-child black, with boots, a hair-do that had looked as if she'd stuck her finger in an electric socket and the kind of make-up job designed to give doting uncles nightmares.

Today her fine skin had been left to shine unadorned—well, almost unadorned—her hair was looped neatly back with a thick bow and she was wearing a full-skirted flower-print dress, with neat low-heeled pumps on her feet. The effect had been finished off with pearl studs in her ears, white gloves and a Kelly bag.

She was also carrying an exquisite posy of cream rosebuds, which presumably were in the nature of a peace offering and the reason for her call. Unlike princes, princesses apparently did it in person. With flowers.

'Nice outfit, Your Highness,' Laura said, with a grin of genuine appreciation for the effort involved. If the girl's career in the family business hadn't been mapped out from birth, she would have made a fine actress. She'd already had a demonstration of her talent last night when she'd feigned a broken ankle. This was different. 'Very Audrey Hepburn,' she said. 'You need an urchin cut to be truly authentic, of course, and perhaps you overdid it with the white gloves—no one wears white gloves now and they smack of caricature—but impressive nonetheless.'

The Princess grinned back, clearly delighted with this response. 'Xander said I had to dress appropriately.'

'And you went for *Roman Holiday*. Good choice. It's a great movie, but forgive me if I don't curtsey. My mother was an American and I'm a natural republican. With a small R.' She held the door open. 'Do you want to come in and say your piece?'

Princess Katerina stepped over the threshold and waited while Laura closed the door. Then she took a deep breath. 'Miss Varndell, I owe you an apology,' she said gravely. 'I played a very wicked trick on you last night.' And she held out the posy of creamy rosebuds, exquisitely wrapped in layers of coffee and cream tissue. 'I do hope you can forgive me.'

'I've met your uncle,' Laura said, taking the flowers. 'There's nothing to forgive. And, since I've had enough Miss Varndells to last me a lifetime, I'd appreciate it if you called me Laura.' She lifted the rosebuds to her face, breathed in the sweet scent. 'These are lovely. Thank you.' Then, 'I'm just about to make coffee. Would you like some?'

There was a flicker of pleased surprise. 'Really? I'm not disturbing you?'

'Not at all, Your Highness,' Laura assured her. If it had been her uncle that would have been a different story. But it wasn't, and she made a brave effort not to be disappointed. Surprisingly, that was harder than she imagined possible. 'Your timing is excellent.'

Better than excellent. She needed a story. The princess could help, even if it was only by giving her the inside story on being sent home for last night's breakout. Photographs were something else, but this was a start. She could always add her own faintly mocking subtext that cast 'Uncle Xander' in the role of pompous killjoy. There should be plenty of library pictures to match that description.

She ignored a raised eyebrow from her subconscious. A what did he do-to-you? look.

Easy. He'd had his footman call her. How pompous was that?

'Come on through to the kitchen while I put these in water,' she said. Then, glancing back at her guest, 'I'm sorry I really can't bring myself to call you ma'am.'

'Not if you want to live,' Princess Katerina agreed, dropping the perfect princess act. 'And one Your Highness goes a long way, too.' She pulled a face. 'It makes me feel like some old dowager. My friends just call me Katie.'

It was Laura's turn to hesitate as, belatedly, she recognised the danger. She already felt more compassion for this young woman than was entirely wise. This was her big chance, she told herself. Her way back. She couldn't afford to go soft. Not this time.

It wasn't as if she'd be spilling any secrets about the girl. She'd already made the diary page of the *Courier* and would be a marked girl for the rest of her stay. Which wouldn't be for long if her uncle had his way. Of course, if Katie had behaved herself last night, accepted that her uncle knew best, there would have been no story.

'Okay, Katie it is,' she said brightly, 'but only if you pull up a stool and relax. I'm not your uncle. We don't stand on ceremony here.' She put on the kettle, then filled a vase and unwrapped the flowers. 'Did he give you a hard time last night?' she asked.

'Xander?' Katie laughed as if the idea was ridiculous. 'He looked stern, growled a bit. He hasn't given me my marching orders yet.'

Laura turned, surprised. 'I got the impression you were going to be on the first available flight to Montorino.'

'Yes, well, it's a bit tricky.'

'Is it?' She didn't believe that His Serene Highness confronted too many obstacles to his will. 'If the flights are all full I'm sure he could put his hands on a private jet.'

'It's not that. The tricky bit is that I'm on a high-profile student exchange programme. European Union stuff. I'm relying on the fact that it will cause even more of a hoo-ha if I'm sent home in disgrace.'

Laura thought it was probably a bit late to worry about that. The 'hoo-ha' had already hit the fan.

Could it be that he'd actually been listening when she'd sounded off at him? Or had the Audrey Hepburn lookalike outfit done the trick? He surely didn't believe Katie had learned her lesson? Reformed overnight? He didn't *look* stupid.

'Anyway,' Katie said, 'I'm on my best behaviour, hoping to convincc him to give me another chance. Meanwhile, I'm grounded until further notice. No public engagements. School and home, with an escort.

One more incident—' She drew a finger, graphically, across her throat. It didn't quite match the single strand of pearls she was wearing.

Biting her lower lip to stop herself from grinning, Laura said, 'That's tough.'

'Well, it has its bright side. It's Royal Ascot next week and Xander has a horse running. He was going to take me. As a treat.' She looked solemn. 'I have this dear little suit in very pale pink that was designed especially for the occasion. And a hat.' She demonstrated its proportions by holding her hands about a foot either side of her head. Then she pulled a face. 'It makes me look like a gangly mushroom.'

The grin won. 'So—it's not all bad news, then?'

Katie giggled. 'Great night out, no boring races. It would have been a total result but for the picture in the paper this morning. I might have got away with just a ticking off, but that was the last straw.'

'Picture?' Laura enquired innocently.

'It was nothing.' She shrugged. 'Well, okay, I suppose it was *something*. We were only at the club for half an hour, but it was long enough for someone to get a picture of me kissing Michael.'

'And Michael is?'

'The brother of one of the girls at school. We met when he picked her up in his sports car.'

No wonder Trevor was mad at her, Laura thought. If she'd phoned the story in straight away he'd have had the story behind the picture. Honours even in the gossip column war.

Still, she was getting there.

'Half an hour—' She frowned. 'It was a lot longer

than that before I got a call to say you were safely home.'

'Oh, well, Xander didn't know about the picture, fortunately, so I was allowed to stay out as long as we left the club and adjourned to somewhere that didn't need ID. No music. No dancing.' She grinned. 'Just Michael.'

'What happened to the others?'

'They were all older so they stayed at the club. Which was fine.'

'I'll bet.' So, Prince Alexander *had* been listening. How he must be wishing he hadn't. 'Pity you didn't wait until you were there before you kissed Michael.'

Pity someone had had a camera turned on them. That was what happened when she tried to do someone a good turn. When her conscience insisted she wait until the girl was safely home before contacting the paper. Her story had been stolen right out from under her.

Worse, she had to admit that Alexander Orsino did know best.

'Xander didn't yell at me,' Katie assured her. 'He just gave me the newspaper so I would understand that he wasn't some old misery trying to stop my fun. And why I'm not allowed out on my own again until he's sure he can trust me.' She gave a very unprincesslike shrug. 'Which basically means the rest of my life.'

'Tough break,' Laura said with feeling.

'What's really tough is that no one is really interested in me. What they really want is Xander caught on camera kissing some gorgeous girl. If he'd just be a little less of the Prince and a little more of the playboy, now that *would* be a story.' She drooped over the breakfast bar. 'And I could get a life.'

'He doesn't have anyone for—' Laura she made a vague gesture that in no way betrayed the way her heart was hammering against her ribs '—kissing?'

'Xander? Once upon a time maybe. Unfortunately, he's far too busy running Montorino for anything that frivolous these days.'

'Too bad.'

'I just hope he gets over it quickly. Missing Ascot is a bonus, but I really wanted to go to Wimbledon with him, meet the tennis stars. Don't you just love the legs on those men?'

'Totally,' Laura said. 'But I wouldn't mention the legs to your uncle. I don't think it would help soften his attitude.'

'You seem to have him all worked out.'

'Do I?'

Laura laid out a couple of cups, trying hard not to be distracted by the thought that Prince Alexander had the kind of powerful wrists that suggested he'd be a great tennis player. If he ever had the time.

She'd got a close-up of them when he'd been cleaning the graze on her face. He had good hands. Not soft....

'Well, I'm glad you had fun last night,' she said, dragging her mind back to the present. 'After such an unpromising start. You weren't hurt at all? When I flattened you? I have a feeling I'm the one who should be apologising—'

'No.' Katie's unexpected blush was of the same era as the print frock. 'Actually, I think you were terribly brave. If I'd been a real burglar—'

'Forget brave. The word is stupid. You know, if you'd told me what you were doing last night I would have looked the other way while you legged it.'

'Would you?'

'I was your age once. Centuries ago.'

Katie giggled. 'You're really nice. I don't suppose you'd consider kissing Xander, would you? Somewhere really public? That would really take the heat off me.'

Laura, taken completely by surprise, needed a second or two to catch her breath before she could think of a coherent answer. Kiss him? Now, there was a thought.

Katie, fortunately, took her hesitation for politeness.

'No, of course not. Silly question. I suppose he's pretty much past the age where anyone would fancy him. I mean, okay, he's a prince and everything, and there is a certain type of woman who finds that whole power trip a turn-on, but Xander hates that.'

Laura, her hands just a little shaky as she took some cream from the fridge and placed it on the table, decided that she shouldn't be having this conversation with his seventeen-year-old niece. No matter how tempted she was.

Then, because it seemed like a good idea to change the subject, and because it had been bothering her, she said, 'Your uncle said you'd apologise, but I expected a phone call. How did you know where I live?'

This was a problem. If her story about the princess's unorthodox exit from her uncle's house had appeared in her own paper this morning, she'd have had not Princess Katerina but His Serene Highness on her doorstep, forcing her to eat her words about his niece living a normal life.

She'd bet her new laptop that he wouldn't have sent the footman. The thought was more appealing than it should have been.

'He didn't send you home in the Rolls?' Katie asked.

'No—' She stopped as there was a further summons on the doorbell. 'Is this your watchdog, wondering what's happened to you?' she asked.

'No, it's her day off. Karl is doing double duty this morning—driver and prisoner escort. But he's more concerned about the car getting clamped than me behaving badly, so I gave him my word I wouldn't do anything stupid.'

And he'd believed her?

'Then it'll be my upstairs neighbour looking for coffee. I'll tell him he's out of luck.'

Her first thought on opening the door was that this couldn't be happening to her. Her second was that she really would have to get one of those spyhole things so that she could see who was there before she opened the door. Her third was a word the princess had used last night. Just after she'd hit the cobbles.

'My niece—' Prince Alexander said, apparently somewhat lost for words himself as he took in her *dishabille* '—has a mind like a sieve.' He was carrying the jacket she'd placed under the girl's head the night before and which she'd obviously decided it was safer to take with her than abandon in the mews lane in case it was stolen.

Thoughtful of her.

It had been cleaned and pressed and was now on a

clothes hanger. Which at least explained how he knew where she lived. There was bound to have been a used envelope in the pocket. Probably several. She recycled them for her shopping lists. Doing her bit to save the planet.

Had she said she was stupid? Make that brainless.

'Well, thank you for taking so much trouble.' About to say that he shouldn't have, she realised that he hadn't. Someone else had been put to that bother. 'And for bringing it back.' At least he'd done that. 'You shouldn't have made a special trip.'

'It was no trouble.'

No, of course it wasn't. All he'd had to do was pick up the phone and summon the chauffeur. No waiting for buses or being scrunched up against the plebs on the underground. 'I just meant that you could have sent your, um, *footman*—'

'I wanted to thank you again. Myself. Make sure there was no lasting damage.'

'Oh, right. Well, as you can see, I'm fine.'

He took a moment to check this out for himself before he said, 'Yes.'

Yes? Just, 'yes'? What did that mean?

Then, 'And, while I didn't travel by public transport, I did drive myself.' This was accompanied by the faintest smile which, since he rationed them like a miser, tended—as she'd noticed last night—to have a rather dramatic effect on her breathing.

'Really?' The word came out in a breathless little rush of surprise.

'I *can* drive.'

'Of course you can,' she said quickly.

'And the, um, footman was busy.'

Now he was laughing at her. And her breath deserted her completely. Again.

'The coffee's ready.' Katie came to an abrupt halt when she saw her uncle. 'Xander? What on earth are you doing here?'

Laura felt rather odd as Prince Alexander continued to hold her gaze; it was like that instant when a high-speed lift begins to descend. A momentary feeling of weightlessness, allied with a sensation that everything inside her body had shifted. Then he looked over her head and answered his niece.

'You forgot to return Miss Varndell's jacket,' he said. 'I thought she might need it.'

'Right,' she said, looking from him to Laura and then back again, her expression suddenly thoughtful.

'It was not all you forgot,' he said abruptly.

'If you're talking about that hideous brooch,' Katie said, pulling a face as he took a velvet-covered box from his pocket, held it up for her to see, 'I didn't forget it. I gave you an opportunity to think again.'

He frowned. 'About the Order of Merit?' Katie continued. 'The ribbon is the loveliest blue, Laura. A perfect match for your eyes. With an enamelled miniature of Great-Grandpa. You wear it on your shoulder at formal—'

'Thank you, Katie.'

She shrugged as her uncle cut her short. 'It's a lot nicer than that brooch, anyway.'

Embarrassed, and very conscious that she wasn't dressed to receive anyone, let alone a royal personage, Laura took the jacket from him and held it modestly in front of her.

'Won't you come in?' she asked, backing up the hall to give him room to step inside her tiny hallway.

'We're in Laura's kitchen,' Katie said. 'Come on through.' She didn't wait to see if he was follow ing her.

Her kitchen! He'd probably never been in his own palatial kitchens. Oh, well. 'Please, do join us,' she said. Adding somewhat belatedly, 'Your Highness.'

'Thank you.' He was still holding the velvet box as if wishing he'd never set eyes on it.

'Shall I take that?'

'It is simply a small token of my thanks,' he said, unexpectedly awkward as he gave it to her.

As she tucked her jacket beneath her arm, her wrap slipped from her shoulder. Since she didn't have a hand to spare, she had no choice but to ignore it and open the box. The brooch, a bright gold oval cartouche enclosing an ornately cut coat of arms, was not large but very heavy. And it wasn't hideous. Far from it. It had been made by a craftsman from fine gold. But it wasn't in any way personal and she suspected it was the royal equivalent of a corporate gift.

'I'll treasure it,' she said gravely. Then, when one of those devilish eyebrows rose a fraction, suggesting he knew exactly what she was thinking, she said, 'I'm sure you'd be more comfortable in the sitting room.'

Xander had already stepped far beyond the bounds of protocol by calling unannounced at Laura Varndell's apartment. Now he was here, he had no intention of being diverted to sit in state in her sitting room.

'The kitchen is perfectly acceptable.'

'Oh, right. Well, if you'll just excuse me, I'd, um, better hang up my jacket.'

Laura backed through a door, opening it just wide enough for her to squeeze through. Even so, he caught a glimpse of a colourful but crumpled patchwork quilt that had slipped to the floor, suggesting a restless night.

'I'll put on something a little more—'

Her voice trailed away as if she realised that it might not be wise to draw further attention to what she was—or wasn't—wearing. He'd spent what seemed like a lifetime practising control of his facial expressions, keeping his thoughts to himself, so even though he wanted to smile he did not.

'I thought it was someone else at the door…'

'Please, take your time, Laura. It won't hurt Katie to practise her hostess skills.'

'Right,' she said again. Then the door closed between them. He remained where he was just long enough to hear her muffled wail of dismay.

Then he smiled.

CHAPTER FOUR

KATIE, who had her mobile phone in her hand, flipped it closed as he slid on to a stool beside her in Laura's little kitchen. 'What on earth do you find to talk about?' he asked.

'Nothing. I just had a text from Michael. Asking me if I'd like to go to the cinema tonight.'

'Michael? That's the boy in the photograph? The one who was kissing you?'

'You make it sound as if he was committing treason.'

'Who said he wasn't?'

'What?'

'I don't think anyone's been executed for kissing a princess for several hundred years in Montorino,' he said. 'But you might like to draw his attention to the fact that the law is still on the statute book.'

'Oh. You were joking.'

'Very nearly,' he admitted.

'Coffee?' she asked. He nodded. 'No milk, no sugar,' she said, passing it to him. 'No frills. Just the way you like it.'

Katie's chatter washed over him as his mind refused to let go of the image that had assaulted him as Laura had opened the door. He wasn't averse to frills in the right place.

The ripple of lace and velvet ribbon on the edge of her wrap, exquisitely framing a hint of cleavage, had seemed about perfect. Before she'd realised that he wasn't the person she'd been expecting and had pulled it closer about her.

'So what do you think, Xander? Am I brilliant, or what?'

'Or what,' he murmured absently, his thoughts still engaged on the curve of Laura's shoulder. The wrap had slipped as she'd juggled her jacket so that she could open the gift he'd brought her.

Who had she been expecting?

'Sorry, I'm not usually so tardy but I had a late night,' Laura said, pausing in the doorway. She'd tied her pale hair back with a scarf, still damp at the ends from what must have been the fastest shower in history, before throwing on a pair of jeans and a loose-fitting white linen shirt that hung below her hips. She shrugged. 'But then you know all about that.'

Before he could answer, Katie butted in.

'Laura, I've had the greatest idea, and Xander agrees with me.'

He did? He turned to look at her but she was cradling her cup between her hands, avoiding his eyes. Up to something.

'What we need is a diversion.'

A diversion?

'A diversion?' Laura voiced his own unspoken query.

'Something to take everyone's mind off that photograph. The one in the newspaper,' she added, in case either of them should be in any doubt.

'Are you sure you want to remind me about that?'

'It's not going to end there, is it? I mean, you know

what it's going to be like. There were photographers outside the house this morning.'

That got his attention. 'There were none when I left.'

'Of course not. They followed me. *I'm* the story. Didn't you see them outside here when you arrived?'

'Here?' He bit back an expletive as he swung round to look up at the window of the semi-basement kitchen which gave an interesting view of the street up to about knee-height and which was no help at all.

Katie lifted her lashes and Laura caught the look she flashed at her. Far from pleading, it had all the assurance of someone born with the Orsino blood flowing through her veins. It said—no, it positively commanded—*follow my lead.* And it occurred to Laura that telling the girl she'd have looked the other way last night might not have been entirely wise.

'I imagine they took photographs of you, too,' she said to her uncle. 'I wonder what they'll make of that.' She poured another coffee with cool aplomb. 'Milk, Laura? Sugar?'

'Just as it comes, thank you.'

'No one took photographs because there was no one outside when I arrived,' Prince Alexander said. He sounded quite certain, but he didn't look entirely happy.

Katie followed his example, glancing at the window as if to check. Then she shrugged. 'No? Oh, well. Maybe they'd got what they wanted and left. Or maybe they're knocking on doors trying to find out who lives here. Who we're visiting. I'm sorry, Laura. This is my fault for forgetting your jacket. It's going to cause you all kinds of bother.' She craned her neck to get a better look at the street. 'Who's that getting out of a car, now? Do you know him?'

No, she really wasn't going along with this. She'd already caused enough damage. 'I can't see.' On the point of declaring herself firmly on the side of the grown-ups she saw, from her better vantage point, someone get out of a car on the far side of the road. It was a photographer from her own newspaper. 'Oh, good grief.' She turned to Prince Alexander. 'I'm afraid Katie's right. That's—' About to blurt out the man's name, she stopped herself. 'That's someone with a camera.'

'Well, then, if they didn't get you on the way in, they'll get you on the way out,' Katie said. 'What a nightmare.' She didn't look *that* upset. 'It looks as if you're going to be a diversion whether you want to be one or not, Laura,' she said, the little sigh of regret not entirely disguising her evident satisfaction. 'Once word gets out that Xander visited you in your apartment my little escapade will be completely forgotten. This will be siege city.'

'But I'll explain,' she began. And then stopped, unable to believe that she'd even said that. 'Or perhaps not.'

'Never apologise, never explain,' Prince Alexander agreed, somewhat wearily. 'It only makes things worse.'

'Yes,' she said. Thinking that he wouldn't be sitting in her kitchen, drinking her coffee, if he knew she was on the side that made it worse. 'You should have stuck with your first thought and sent the footman.'

That, at least, raised a smile. 'Did that offend you?'

'I'm sorry?' She went for innocent.

He wasn't fooled. 'Last night. You think I should have called you myself,' he persisted.

There was no point in denying it. He knew. 'Well, if the situation had been reversed I'd have made the effort,' she admitted. 'Even if I had a footman to run my errands. But I imagine you had better things to do. Running a country must be a full-time job if you will insist on doing it all yourself—'

'I do not have a choice—'

'Actually,' Katie cut in, swiftly, 'it's not all bad news.'

They both turned to look at her.

'Now you two are a hot item, I'm off the hook. If you took Laura to Ascot in my place, no one would remember I existed and I could get on with being just an ordinary student for three months.'

She'd called the newspaper herself, Laura thought in the apparently endless silence that met this suggestion. The little madam has taken the opportunity to stage-manage a little embarrassment for Uncle Xander. Once he was on the front page who would worry what Katie did?

'No,' Prince Alexander said finally, dragging her back to reality. 'It's out of the question.'

Of course it was. Unthinkable.

Why?

'I cannot possibly make Miss Varndell the subject of idle gossip just so that you can go to the cinema with your boyfriend,' he finished.

Oh, right. That was why. Nothing to do with her being a peasant and him being a prince. He was just being chivalrous. Noble.

What a nuisance. Poor Katie. Poor her. Just when she looked like getting the story she wanted. The one she'd already promised Trevor.

She'd happily weather a little gossip for the opportunity to get close to Prince Alexander Michael George Orsino. A lot of gossip.

She was prepared to suffer for her career.

Really.

Quite a lot.

'Actually,' Laura said. And suddenly she was the one who was the focus of two pairs of eyes. One hopeful, the other expressionless. 'In view of my somewhat outspoken comments last night—' and please, please let him overlook her most recent outspoken comments on his undemocratic leadership style '—it would seem the very least I can do is provide a little cover so that Katie can have some breathing space. A chance to be ordinary for a week or two.'

Katie had the sense to keep quiet. In fact, the quiet went on so long that Laura was certain His Serene Highness knew exactly what she was doing. Could see the feature her imagination was already planning.

The noise of the fridge starting up broke the silence, and she jumped.

'It would not disrupt your personal life?' he asked at last.

'My personal life?' Phooey to her personal life. She didn't have a personal life to speak of. She'd been too busy trying to establish her career. And to date failing miserably. A situation that would change dramatically if he would just ask her.

'Your job?' he persisted.

Help!

'For heaven's sake, Xander. Just ask her. If it's a problem, she'll say no.' Behind Xander's back Katie silently mouthed, *Say, yes!*

At that moment, with everything to gain, Laura knew that she couldn't go through with it.

'No,' she said, ignoring Katie's anguished look. 'Forget I said that. You're absolutely right, it's quite impossible.'

Whatever had she been thinking? He was a prince, for heaven's sake. She wasn't the kind of girl that princes escorted to premier events of the English social calendar. She read the papers. The gossip mags.

The girl on his arm had to be a blue-blooded aristocrat like himself. A society beauty. Or, failing that, a movie star. A supermodel at the very least.

Not some little nobody who couldn't even hold down a job.

But wouldn't it make a great story…?

She put temptation behind her. 'It really wouldn't do, Your Highness,' she said, making her point with his title. 'I'd love to help you out, Katie, but, no. It really wouldn't do.'

Xander knew he should accept her decision. That she was right.

But Katie was right, too. And it would deal with that tiresome photograph very satisfactorily…

'On the contrary, I believe it would do very well. I'd be honoured if you'd accompany me to Royal Ascot, Laura.'

'Honoured?'

She sounded vaguely put out. Maybe it had sounded a bit forced. A good-mannered man backed into a corner. He hadn't meant it that way. In fact he'd be—

'Delighted?' he offered. 'Please come.'

Prince Alexander's expression hadn't changed, but there was something about the eyes, a suggestion of warmth that hadn't been there before, and Laura's heart unexpectedly flipped over.

Please come

Oh, good grief. This was it, she thought, slightly numb at this sudden turn of events. And more than faintly uneasy about what Katie was up to. She was certainly up to something.

But what the heck? It wasn't her concern. She'd worry about that later. She had a date with Prince Alexander Michael George Orsino. Forget some mini-diary piece that might, albeit grudgingly, have got her her job back. She was on the point of the story of a lifetime. The story she'd set out to get, what was more. This was colour supplement stuff and Trevor McCarthy had better be prepared to do some serious grovelling if he wanted it. Make her an offer she couldn't refuse.

'Well, if you're sure about being delighted...' She matched his almost smile with one of her own. Firmly buttoning down the urgent desire to grin wildly that was welling up from somewhere deep inside.

Thank you, Jay! she wanted to shout. You are just totally brilliant!

Even as her head was running away with excitement she could practically hear her aunt sternly cutting through her nonsense as she said, 'Don't make a mess of this opportunity, my girl. It's the chance of a lifetime. You're giving him what he wants. Now is the time to ask for something in return.'

What? Oh, no. She couldn't, shouldn't. But this wasn't about the kind of day out that she would tell her grandchildren about. This was work.

Deep breath.

Go for it.

'...I'd be equally delighted to accept.' She left a pause long enough for her heart to pound against her chest twice. 'But I'm afraid I do have one condition.'

'Only one?'

He'd reverted to the ice man. Clearly no one in the history of the world had ever put a condition on accepting an invitation from an Orsino. She wanted to say, Sorry, forget that, I didn't mean it. I want to come with you, get to know you just for me...

He waited. Her mouth dried.

Too late to call back the words, go back to the warmth.

'Nothing onerous,' she said, her attempt at keeping her voice light coming out just plain squeaky. 'But if Katie is going to have a break from being a princess, Your Highness, I think you should have a taste of "ordinary" life, too.'

Laura caught her breath as, behind Prince Alexander, Katie's mouth dropped open in the kind of shocked reaction that not even a well-trained princess was able to disguise.

It was as if she was determined to sabotage her career. This time she'd completely blown it. Thrown it all away. Not content with a workmanlike piece on spending the day with Prince Alexander at Ascot, she'd wanted more. A lot more.

What on earth had she been *thinking*?

Oh, *that* was easy.

She hadn't been thinking at all. It was always the same. She disengaged her brain and leapt in with both feet.

Or maybe not.

Maybe her feet, for once, knew best.

Ascot—delightful though it would be to swan around the royal enclosure as the guest of Prince Alexander—wasn't going to help her career.

The truth of the matter was that if she appeared at Ascot with His Serene Highness, she would *be* the story. That was the whole point of the invitation, after all. Which was fair enough. She could live with that. But she was entitled to something in return.

The story she'd rashly told Trevor she was going to deliver.

The story on which her entire future depended. The one with pictures.

Alexander Orsino knew that he had been handbagged.

By Katie, who had managed to manipulate him because he hadn't been paying attention—distracted by Laura Varndell in a state of undress. And by Laura, who in any state at all was a distraction few men would be able to resist.

It was why he was here, after all. Responding to the memory of vivid eyes, a mouth that was quick to smile. A mouth that wasn't afraid to tell him exactly what its owner thought.

It was why he had not sent her jacket—or the brooch—with a messenger. Never able to fool himself, he was not about to start now. He had wanted to take a second look, get another charge from the energy she'd brought with her into his home. And his forgetful niece had given him the opportunity.

But it was time for him to regain control.

He glanced at his watch. 'Katie, I don't think you should keep Karl waiting any longer,' he said, without taking his eyes off Laura. 'Not if you are going to get packed in time to catch the afternoon flight.'

'Pack?' Katie's eyes widened in shock. 'But I thought—'

'My hope that you might avoid further attention was clearly a forlorn one.' He indicated the window. 'The photograph of you has already fuelled media attention. The press will keep taking photographs of you and keep rehashing last night's story. It is not going to go away, so you will have to.'

'But you said—' Katie, on the point of arguing, took one look at his face and realised that there was no point. Instead, hiding her hurt under a careless shrug, she turned to Laura. 'Can you believe it? One kiss and I'm banished. I might as well become a nun.' Then, remembering her manners, 'Thank you for coffee, Laura. And for trying to help.'

'I'm *so* sorry, Katie—'

She seemed genuinely distressed, he thought. Blamed herself. But Katie was fair.

'Don't be. It's not your fault. Just be glad you have a life.' His niece saved her ire for him, glaring at him as she picked up her bag, biting back tears, refusing to let them fall before she turned and almost ran from the apartment.

Laura flinched as the door slammed. 'Did you have to be so cruel?' she demanded, forgetting all about addressing him as Your Highness in that slightly arch manner that was just short of insolent. That suggested she thought the whole title thing was ridiculous.

'I'm not being cruel.' He moved towards the window, watching as the waiting photographer called out to Katie, snapping her tearful face as she looked up before climbing into the back of the car. 'Far from it. Do you see?' he said, inviting her to follow his gaze.

She left it just long enough to allow him the full impact of her disapproval before she glanced out of the window.

'Tomorrow,' he continued, 'there will be a report in the press that Princess Katerina has been sent home in disgrace after the nightclub incident. That photograph will confirm just how upset she is. No one will doubt it.'

'And?'

'And with luck the photographer will follow her now so that I can leave undetected.'

'You mean you're sending her home in tears simply to avoid having your immaculate reputation sullied by the press?' she demanded.

'My reputation is neither here nor there. I don't want you having to fight your way out of a front door blocked by newsmen demanding to know what I was doing here.'

'Oh.'

'Her banishment isn't permanent. Next week she can fly back to London without the VIP treatment. Economy class perhaps would be best. Very ordinary.' Her eyes narrowed but she wasn't quite ready to smile. 'I will arrange for her to stay with her mother's old nanny and, provided she does nothing to draw attention to herself, she can return to school on Monday like any ordinary girl. Live anonymously for the next three months. Take the bus. Even go to the cinema with some boy called Michael who has yet to learn that kissing a girl is something not to be shared with the rest of the world.'

He looked down at her, found himself distracted by the way a strand of her hair was sliding over an ear that was today decorated with a little gold teddy bear. Had to physically stop himself from tucking it back into place. From kissing the frown from her lovely face.

'Isn't that what you wanted for her?' he asked, to distract himself.

'Well, yes. But you could have told her that,' Laura said, still indignant, if slightly confused. 'She's a very convincing actress.'

'Sometimes acting isn't enough, Laura. Sometimes you have to feel the pain.' He shrugged. 'So, perhaps I wanted to make a point, too. Remind her what will happen if she's stupid enough to go clubbing again. She won't get another chance.'

'That's harsh.'

'Just reality. One mistake might be forgotten if there's a distraction. Two will make her a target. I'm sure she'll get the point.'

'Maybe. I still think you should have told her.'

'I will. I'll call her tomorrow,' he replied, leaving her in no doubt that the subject was closed. 'In the meantime we have to make sure that the press have something more interesting to focus on.'

'We?'

'Ascot? You did volunteer,' he pointed out. 'You

can, of course, change your mind. I am certain Katie will understand why she cannot return—'

Now he had her attention. Her lovely eyes flashed as they focused on him.

'No! No, really. If it'll help Katie—' Then, not quite able to meet his eyes, she said, 'I'm sorry I said that—about you being cruel. She's fortunate to have someone who'll give her the chance to have her "ordinary" life, however briefly.'

'She has three months. I hope she makes the most of it. It will have to last her the rest of her life,' he said, his mouth tightening as he said it. Angry about that. 'My time is rather more constrained. I have a week at the most.' He turned to her. 'So, Laura, tell me, what do you have in mind?'

'Sorry?'

'You offered me a taste of ordinary life. A holiday from affairs of state. The dreary social round of receptions, galas, official dinners.'

'I never said they were dreary,' she said.

'Oh, but they are, Laura. Believe me, they are.' Although she would undoubtedly liven things up. They might even become enjoyable— 'So,' he said, 'if the invitation is still open I am at your command. Or do you believe I am not worth the effort? That I am beyond help?'

The comic look of blank astonishment on her face made him want to laugh out loud.

'Are you free this afternoon?' he pressed.

'This afternoon,' she repeated, as if unfamiliar with the words. 'As in *today*?'

'We have no time to waste. After Ascot,' he pointed out, 'you won't have an ordinary life to share with me. You'll be part of the circus. However briefly.'

'No. I suppose not. Although now that you've made Katie invisible there's really no need—'

She stopped, perhaps realising that she was just about to talk herself out of an invitation to one of the social events of the year. She was safe. He wasn't about to let that happen. This had nothing to do with Katie. He was doing this for himself.

'Can you just take time off like that?' she asked. 'What about your official engagements?'

'A diplomatic virus?' he offered. 'Or perhaps a touch of exhaustion?'

'No one will believe that.'

'You think anyone will dare to say so to my face?'

She blushed. 'No, I suppose not.'

'It will only take one journalist with the curiosity to follow up Katie's story and discover the truth to ruin the whole thing for her. We need to redirect their attention. If Katie is to return, Ascot is not negotiable. Which is why I'm accepting your terms,' he said. 'You get to make your point. Starting this afternoon.'

Laura seemed momentarily lost for words. Which he thought was probably a first. It didn't last. 'If your country can spare you,' she said, 'my afternoon is yours.'

'It will stagger on without me for a few hours,' he assured her. The paperwork would pile up, but it would do that anyway. 'What about your own job?'

'Job?'

'I assume, being ordinary, you do have a job?'

'If I had a job I'd be there right now,' she pointed out. 'I'm, um, between appointments.'

'How fortunate for me. I'll pick you up at about three, after I have taken Katie to the airport. I should organise her flight. May I use your telephone?'

'Help yourself.'

While he called his aide, Laura crossed to the window and looked up at the street.

'Is your car the big black convertible?' she asked, when he rang off and joined her to check that the photographer had, indeed, followed Katie.

'Is that a problem?'

'We should all have such problems.' As she turned to look at him the sunlight touched her hair, lighting up the soft curls that were now hell-bent on escaping her high-speed attempt at control, turning them into a silver-gilt halo. 'But it isn't exactly *ordinary*.'

'No,' he said, not looking at the car. 'Not ordinary at all.'

'Better leave it at home this afternoon. It'll attract attention.' She frowned. 'That photographer might run a check on the numberplate to find out who owns it.'

'It is registered to a company,' he said.

'Montorino plc?'

'Near enough. I take your point.'

'Better take the bus as well. The number forty-two stops just along the road.' And she caught her lower lip to stop a smile from breaking out, her teeth tugging at the soft pink flesh, giving his body ideas that his brain knew to be ill-advised.

His brain wasn't listening. He didn't want to use public transport. He wanted to drive them both out into the country and get lost somewhere without telephones or newspapers until next week, when they'd put in an appearance at Ascot and he would be forced to come back down to earth.

'Give it a try,' she pressed, when he didn't respond. 'It'll be a new experience for you.'

'I can't wait.'

Laura closed the door, leaned against it. Groaned. What had she done?

Got herself a story, that was what, she told herself firmly. A career-enhancing story. At least she'd got the makings of one.

Get it right and Trevor McCarthy would welcome her back with open arms.

Get it right and she'd be taken seriously.

And what about Prince Alexander? She pushed away the niggling voice of a conscience that would intrude at the most inconvenient moments.

What about him? He was one of the richest men on earth. He had everything a man could dream of.

All she wanted was the job she'd set her heart on from the moment she'd been able to read her mother's articles—had understood what Jay did. It wasn't such an impossible dream. She was prepared to work hard. Wasn't asking to be rich, or famous.

Prince Alexander owned a whole country, for heaven's sake, with his own palace to live in during the week and a fairytale castle in the country for weekends and vacations. A mansion in London. Sports cars. A yacht, in all probability.

The last thing in this world he needed was her sympathy.

What about that young maid who was clearly terrified out of her wits by him? What about a country governed by an autocrat?

The last thing he *deserved* was her sympathy.

He didn't give a fig about her privacy. He knew that after Ascot she'd have every paparazzo in London camped on her doorstep, yet he'd practically blackmailed her into accepting his invitation. Making it clear that if she backed out Katie would be staying in Montorino.

So. That was clear, then. No problem. She could do this. He'd have his distraction and she'd file her story to run on the day the pictures appeared of them both at Ascot.

CHAPTER FIVE

ALEXANDER knew he should not be doing this; there were a hundred things demanding his attention. But then there always were. And a deal was a deal. Laura was compromising her privacy to give Katie some peace. The least he could do in return was indulge her determination to show him what she thought he was missing.

He found himself smiling at that. It would be interesting to compare notes when she'd experienced life from his point of view. He thought a little public transport might go a long way once she'd tasted the comfort of a chauffeur-driven Rolls.

It was, after all, only fair that she should give him a chance to convert her to his point of view. Something he hadn't mentioned when he'd accepted her challenge.

Then, as he searched through his wardrobe for something suitably pedestrian to wear, he wondered if she'd have the same problem with clothes for Ascot. All the other women in their party would be dressed in *haute couture*. Would she be offended if he offered to underwrite the expense?

Without a doubt, he decided.

And was torn between the conflicting reactions of pleasure and regret. He was attracted by her frankness, her honesty, artlessness. All those qualities that meant she'd tell him to keep his *haute couture*.

But it would have been a pleasure to dress Laura in the softest silks, hand-stitched linen, shoes fit for a princess.

He caught sight of his reflection in a tall cheval mirror and pulled a self-mocking face. Correction. Dressing her had been the furthest thing from his mind.

Just as well she would never allow him such self-indulgence.

'Shopping?'

'Shopping,' Laura confirmed. 'I'm sorry it's nothing more exciting.'

Prince Alexander had arrived exactly on time, having taken only partial heed of her advice and been dropped off by a taxi at the end of the street. At least he was wearing the standard uniform of the off-duty male, the kind of classless clothes that would blend in anywhere.

Unfortunately His Highness, strikingly tall, strikingly broad-shouldered, was incapable of looking ordinary even in jeans. Or maybe it was just the way they clung to his waist, his backside, thighs, as if moulded to him, that lifted her pulse-rate. The faded wear creases were all in the right places, too.

How had they got that way?

The man in the photograph on the cover of *Celebrity* magazine didn't look as if he'd ever heard of denim, let alone worn it on a regular basis.

Dragging her mind back to the business in hand, she said, 'Us ordinary folk have to eat, too.' Her nerves were wound up to snapping point, making her sharper than she'd meant to be. 'But with us it's a do-it-yourself thing. First we shop. Then we cook. Then we eat.'

'No problem,' he replied, politely ignoring her edginess. 'I just wondered if I'd gone a bit too down-market in my attempt to blend in, but clearly your idea of shopping doesn't coincide with Katie's.'

'We're not going anywhere near Knightsbridge, if that's what you mean. Someone would be sure to recognise you there. Even wearing jeans.'

It occurred to her that she was giving his hips entirely too much attention and she forced her gaze upwards. Met those disconcertingly dark eyes head on.

What was he *thinking*?

'You'll fit right in at the local market,' she said.

At least his clothes would. Prince Alexander would always stand out from the crowd, turn heads, no matter how 'down-market' he dressed. He might be wearing the clothes of the average man in the street, but he still had the bearing of an aristocrat. A prince.

She'd just have to rely on the sheer improbability of His Serene Highness touring the local street market, apparently picking out vegetables for his supper, to keep him incognito.

She'd originally settled on a visit to the supermarket as the most ordinary thing she could think of. The up side of having him push a trolley round the shelves would, unfortunately, be more than offset by the fact that his photograph was on the front page of this week's *Celebrity* magazine, prominently displayed on the news-stand just by the entrance.

There was a head-turning quality about him that she wasn't prepared to risk in such close proximity to his official likeness.

Besides, there was more light out of doors in the street market; she'd get better pictures. All she had to do was keep her nerve for a couple of hours.

And why not?

He'd asked for this, she reminded herself. She'd tried to step back.

Fortunately for her, he hadn't let her.

'We'd better get on,' she said. 'I don't know how much time you can spare.'

'I've given myself the rest of the day off. On good advice.'

'Oh?' Then, 'Oh!' He meant hers. 'Right,' she said, just a bit flustered. 'Well, in that case maybe you'd like to stay and eat…' She was rarely short of words, but he just had to look at her that way and her mouth dried.

'What we've bought?' he finished for her. 'At the market?'

'Mmm.'

'That sounds…'

This time he was the one lost for words. And who could blame him? Shopping and cooking wouldn't feature prominently in his average day. Year. Decade.

'Ordinary?' she offered.

'For you, maybe. Not for me.'

'No. I suppose not.' Then, 'You don't have anything more exciting planned for this evening?'

'A notice will appear in ''Court and Social'' tomorrow to the effect that I am suffering from a slight cold and have cancelled my engagements for the rest of the week.'

'You really did it?'

'It wasn't much of a wrench. My life isn't all caviar

and champagne,' he said, with a wry smile in response to her little dig at him. 'In fact, it's rarely either of those things. All I have to look forward to tonight is an evening with a report from my finance minister.'

She wasn't quite sure whether he was joking, whether she was supposed to laugh or not. It occurred to her that, despite the hauteur, the formality of his speech and manners, he was a lot better at this than she was, which was a surprise. That aristocratic nose didn't quite go with teasing. Or maybe it was just part of the defence mechanism. He would be good at guarding himself.

'I consider it my duty to save you from that,' she said, giving him the benefit of the doubt and teasing him back.

'Thank you, Laura.'

'You're very welcome—'

What? What on earth was she going to call him? Sir? Your Highness? Prince Alexander?

'Xander,' he said, proving—unnervingly—that he was perfectly capable of reading her mind when he made the effort.

She frowned, as if she didn't have a clue what he was talking about.

'You were wondering what to call me. You've been having problems with it ever since we met.'

'I have?'

He looked down at her. 'Most people stick with "Your Highness" or "Your Serene Highness" in the first instance, depending upon the formality of the occasion, followed by "Sir". That's the accepted form. Protocol. But you don't approve of titles.'

'How do you know?'

'Because, on the few occasions you've used mine, it sounded like an insult.'

She didn't deny it. 'My mother was an American. I'm a natural republican. With a small R—'

'You don't have to explain. Or apologise, Laura—'

'I wasn't apologising!'

'Just say it.'

'Your Serene Highness'?'

'Xander.'

'Xander,' she repeated, but still feeling as if she'd got a mouthful of cotton wool.

'It's just a name. Like ordinary people have. Don't go self-conscious on me, now. It doesn't suit you.'

'No. It's just that I can't help feeling that I could get locked up in the Tower for being so forward.'

That appeared to amuse him. Brackets formed on either side of his mouth and she caught a glimpse of teeth as he smiled. He should do that more often, she thought.

'You weren't reluctant to give me the benefit of your opinion last night. Or this morning.'

'Mmm? Oh, that's because I have this problem with my mouth. It speaks without thinking. It can get me into a lot of trouble.'

'I don't doubt it.' He picked up her shopping basket and offered it to her. 'However, you're going to have to risk the Tower because if you address me as "Your Serene Highness" in the market,' he said, the smile disappearing as quickly as it had come, 'it will rather give the game away. Won't it?'

'You're right.' He lifted a brow, prompting her to be bold. 'Xander.' She took the basket, trying to ignore the sensation that she'd just stepped over the edge of an abyss. Then she picked up the worn leather shoulder bag sent by Trevor McCarthy, slinging it over her shoulder as casually as she could, holding her breath, waiting for him to pick out the telltale glint of a lens disguised by a chunky rivet. Spot that its matching pair was in fact a shutter release. Which was totally stupid.

Why would Prince Alexander—Xander—even suspect what she was planning?

If he'd had the least idea he wouldn't be here.

'If you're ready?' He opened the kitchen door, standing back for her to precede him. 'Did Katie catch her flight?' she asked, reaching for normality as she headed for the front door.

She'd be fine. It was just nerves, that was all. A little air and her breathing would return to normal.

'With much wailing and gnashing of teeth,' he said, as they took the steps up from her basement flat to the street. 'She reverted to the wild child look in sulky protest for her trip home. Which, since the photographer tailed her all the way to the airport, couldn't have worked out better.'

'When is she coming back?' she asked, attempting the kind of normal conversation they'd have if this *were* a normal conversation. She sounded stilted, hideously false to her own ears.

'At the weekend,' he replied, apparently noticing nothing odd in her manner. But then maybe that was the way people always were around him. 'I've spoken to her mother and she's arranged for Nanny Blake to meet her at the airport and take her home. After that, it's up to Katie.' He glanced up at the tall house they'd just left. 'Have you lived here long?'

'What?'

That did attract a look of surprise.

Oh, good grief. She had to get a grip. That was an ordinary question, she told herself. The kind of question anyone would ask. Only her guilty conscience made it feel like an interrogation.

'Oh, *here*. All my life,' she said, as they began to walk down the street. Xander took the outside, his arm brushing against hers, which made it difficult to concentrate. 'My parents bought the house when I was born. As a base. They travelled a lot, you see. My father was a climber. My mother a travel writer. Once they married they combined their interests. They were rarely home.'

'Tough for you.'

'I never knew anything else.' Nannies, boarding school, Jay. She'd always been there. Had compromised her own career to stay close after the death of her parents. 'They actually met on a plane,' she said. 'When they were killed my father's aunt—my guardian—decided the best thing to do was convert the house into apartments. That way I'd still have my home.' Continuity. Wouldn't have lost everything she knew. 'And an income,' she added.

'Practical woman.'

'Yes. She is. Practical and kind and I owe her so much. She sold her own home, came to live in the garden flat with me so that I could come back in the school holidays. Until I was old enough to live on my own, that is.' He didn't say anything and she pressed on, 'Then she moved up to the next floor.' She smiled. 'The garden flat has its own front door, you see. She thought I should have the freedom to come and go without feeling as if I was being timed in and out.' She grinned. 'At least, that's what she said. I have a feeling she just wanted to see the back of the garden, tiny though it is.'

'How do you feel about gardening?'

'Love it,' she admitted. 'Although it's largely a matter of filling the pots. One day, when I've made my name and I'm rich and famous, I'm going to have a proper garden.' She moved quickly on. 'A couple of girls who work in a bank live on the floor above her. Sean's got the attic studio.'

'Sean?'

'He's an actor. Mostly. When he's not working as a cleaner, or dog walker, or waiter.' She eased her shoulders up into something resembling a shrug. 'When you rang the bell this morning I thought it was him or I'd have put on some clothes.' That hadn't come out quite the way she'd intended. 'Before I opened the door.'

She glanced up but his face was giving nothing away. She knew the technique. Nature abhors a vacuum and people are unnerved by silence. She used it herself. If you just stayed silent long enough the other person would leap in to fill the void.

Knowing it didn't stop her from being unnerved. Or leaping in.

'He usually drops by for coffee.'

Still no response.

If Xander kept this up for long enough she'd probably blurt out her entire life story. Everything. Even her truly embarrassing crush on a waste-of-space pop

The Harlequin Reader Service® — Here's how it works:

Accepting your 2 free books and mystery gift places you under no obligation to buy anything. You may keep the books and gift and return the shipping statement marked "cancel." If you do not cancel, about a month later we'll send you 6 additional books and bill you just $3.34 each in the U.S., or $3.80 each in Canada, plus 25¢ shipping and handling per book and applicable taxes if any.* That's the complete price and — compared to cover prices of $3.99 in the U.S. and $4.50 in Canada — it's quite a bargain! You may cancel at any time, but if you choose to continue, every month we'll send you 6 more books, which you may either purchase at the discount price or return to us and cancel your subscription.

*Terms and prices subject to change without notice. Sales tax applicable in N.Y. Canadian residents will be charged applicable provincial taxes and GST. Credit or debit balances in a customer's account(s) may be offset by any other outstanding balance owed by or to the customer.

BUSINESS REPLY MAIL

FIRST-CLASS MAIL PERMIT NO. 717-003 BUFFALO, NY

POSTAGE WILL BE PAID BY ADDRESSEE

HARLEQUIN READER SERVICE
3010 WALDEN AVE
PO BOX 1867
BUFFALO NY 14240-9952

star when she was fourteen and certainly old enough to have had better taste.

'If I'm still home when he gets up,' she said, a little desperately.

'What do you do?'

'Do?' Her relief that he'd broken his silence was ruined by confusion. 'When I get up?'

'When you're not between "appointments"? How do you plan to make your name and so become rich and famous?'

Oh, sugar! She knew she'd made a mistake as soon as the words had slipped from her mouth. Had hoped she'd covered her gaff.

'You're blushing, Laura.'

Nothing so innocent. It was hot shame at her deception. But if he thought she was blushing she could live with that. Just.

'Well, the thing is—' she began, then stopped, her mind a complete blank.

'Don't tell me,' he said, coming to her rescue.

'You don't want to know?'

'I've guessed.' Her heart stopped. She'd swear it actually stopped beating... 'You're an actress *manqué*?'

What?

'Am I right?'

'Good grief, no!'

She didn't actually groan out loud, but it was close. He'd just given her the perfect excuse to be out of work—the *manqué* covered that very nicely—and available to spend time with him. Instead of grabbing it with both hands she'd leapt on her high horse. Been insulted that he could even think such a thing.

Not that she had anything against the theatre, but she couldn't imagine anything worse than living the self-absorbed life of her top-floor tenant, constantly stressing over the way he looked, the parts his rivals had stolen from under his nose.

She wanted more than that. She wanted to make a difference in this world.

So, what on earth was she doing wasting her time on a royal story?

And what on earth, she wondered, was Jay doing, encouraging her?

She realised that Prince Alexander was waiting for her to tell him what she did that was so much more relevant than Sean. Something that wouldn't give the game away.

'I guess I'm still looking for my own particular niche.' She attempted a smile. 'Something that manages to juggle the enormity of my aspirations with the limits of my talent.'

'Just like everyone else, in fact. But then you're a woman of property,' he said. 'I suppose you can afford to be choosy.' Maybe she was being ultra-sensitive, but he didn't make it sound like anything to be proud of.

'Not everyone gets their own hand-carved niche handed to them at birth,' she snapped right back at him. 'For no other reason than who your father happens to be.' Then, for good measure, 'And because you're a man.'

'Laura—'

'What does your sister feel about that? She is older than you?'

'Five years older,' he admitted.

'And this is the twenty-first century?' She didn't wait for him to answer that one. It was a purely rhetorical question. 'It's not as if there haven't been some pretty successful queens in the past. Women Prime Ministers, even.'

'I take your point, Laura.'

'Okay, so I own a house, but I don't sit around navel gazing all day. Who do you think pays the bills when the roof leaks, or the gutter needs replacing? Rolls up her sleeves when the hall needs a coat of paint?' They were passing the local pizzeria. 'Who do you think has to buckle down and do a little waitressing when the expenses outstrip the income?' Or when she'd messed up the day job. 'Believe me, that's not a career choice.'

'I wasn't criticising.'

'No?' It had surely sounded like it.

'No.' He shrugged. 'Look, maybe I'm being clumsy. I don't often get a chance to meet complete strangers. Not like this.'

He was apologising? She'd just bet that was a new experience for him.

'I'm just trying to get to know you, that's all. My life is an open book, as you've just demonstrated. But you're undiscovered territory.'

'And you're an explorer?'

He half raised his hand in a gesture of self-defence. 'It's beginning to feel like a hack through impenetrable jungle.'

He mustn't think that. He'd start to wonder what she had to hide. She caught a sideways glance. He already was.

'I'm sorry.' She shook her head. 'I didn't mean to

sound so defensive. I guess I'm sensitive about letting the feminist side down. Girls with my kind of education are supposed to be out there, making their mark on life.' Something she had failed to do.

'You went to college?'

'I read English at Oxford,' she admitted. And got a First. But she couldn't tell him that or he'd never believe she hadn't got a proper job, even though it was the truth right now. He might even put two and two together and come up with a big fat four. 'Which makes it worse.'

'You certainly seem to be over-qualified to be a waitress.'

'Possibly. Although, in my opinion, if everyone was forced to wait on tables for at least one week of their life the world would be a kinder place.' Then she gave a what-am-I-to-do? shrug. 'But I didn't want to teach and I hate being stuck in an office.' All true.

'That certainly limits your choices.'

'My most recent employer, while inviting me to explore other career opportunities, suggested I might like to consider child-care.' He lifted a brow, inviting her to elaborate. 'It's a long story,' she said quickly.

'At least you have the freedom to choose,' he said.

'You're saying you'd rather not be the Heir Apparent to Montorino?' It belatedly occurred to her that just because the job was his by birthright, it didn't mean he was happy about it.

'I'm pointing out that you do have a choice,' he said, leaving her question unanswered. 'And that you aren't making it.'

On the point of telling him that he could give up his title and embrace democracy, she took a foot-in-the-mouth check; his opinion of her didn't matter. He was right: she had a choice. Her choice was to be a journalist and it was about time she started acting like one before she offended him so deeply that he caught the next passing bus just to get away from her.

'So what would you have done?' she asked. 'If you'd had the freedom to choose?'

'I have never indulged myself in the luxury of fantasy.'

It was the response of a man who was used to deflecting questions he didn't want to answer. But her readers would really want to know.

She really wanted to know.

'Come on. You must have wanted to be a racing driver, a sportsman of some kind?' she teased. 'All kids do. You're having a day off from being a prince so let your hair down. Dream a little.'

'I'm a lost cause, I'm afraid. A born pragmatist. Totally devoid of fancy.'

So what was he doing here? Playing a part? Pretending to be ordinary. She'd suggested it, implied it went with the whole Ascot deal. But no one had been twisting his arm. She'd have gone with him even if he'd turned down her cheeky condition. He must know that.

So, while he might believe what he was saying, she didn't. A pragmatist wouldn't be walking down this very ordinary road, going to the local street market to buy the ingredients for her supper.

But she didn't challenge him.

'My mistake.' Then, 'It's just round here. I hope we're not too late to get what I want. I usually come in the morning, but I thought you might enjoy it.'

'Late can be good. It's a time for bargains.'

'Excuse me?' she said, giving him a disbelieving look. 'And you would know about that?'

'I know about economics. The perishable stuff will be no good tomorrow so the traders will be selling it off cheap.'

As if to confirm what he said, as they turned the corner one of them began to loudly proclaim his bargains.

'Can you cook, Laura?'

'What?'

'You were threatening to make dinner.'

She stopped, forcing him to do the same. 'And you wondered if you should take the risk? Well, thanks for the vote of confidence.'

He turned to face her. 'I just thought we might try a pizza,' he said gently. 'One that you didn't have to serve.'

There was the suspicion of a smile creasing the corners of his mouth. It was matched by a warmer glow to his eyes. As if the shutters had been lifted. For a moment she forgot to breathe.

'Well?' he prompted.

The shortage of oxygen caused her to feel momentarily dizzy, but when she recovered she lifted her basket and said, 'You wouldn't be trying to wriggle out of shopping, would you?'

She hadn't attempted to offload the basket on to him. She was counting on him carrying it back when it was full. Counting on him being too much of a gentleman to do anything elsc. Onc had to take every photo opportunity.

'Not at all. I just thought I'd rather talk to you over

a simple meal than sit and twiddle my thumbs while you cook.'

Oh, boy. Now, was that a challenge she could resist? Not in a million years.

'Whatever made you think you'd be sitting twiddling anything, Xander? I'm going to cook a green Thai curry the way Jay taught me. And you're going to help.'

'Jay?'

'My great-aunt. The one who lives upstairs. She's travelled a lot, too. And she taught me to cook.'

'And now you're going to teach me?'

He spoke softly, yet there was an edge to his voice. A warning that she was fooling herself if she thought she could teach him anything.

'You're about to become a new man, Xander,' she said, as she finally shook off the nervousness that had apparently paralysed her wits since she'd opened her door to him, and started to enjoy herself. 'Better relax and enjoy it.'

He laughed. 'I don't seem to have much choice,' he said, as she crossed to her favourite stall.

'Hello, Charlie. What's good today?'

'Hello, duchess. You're just in time for a bargain. Bananas half price. Lovely peaches—six for the price of four. I'm a fool to myself.'

'I'll believe you—hundreds wouldn't,' she said, laughing as she handed him her basket. 'I'll take six peaches. No squidgy ones from the bottom, mind. I'm going to poach them and I don't want them disintegrating.'

'I'm cut to the quick that you could even suggest such a thing.'

'Is that so? Well, just make sure you don't bleed over the fruit,' she said, grinning as she picked up a large onion and offered it to Xander.

He took it, looked at it. Then looked at her. 'It's an onion,' he offered.

Charlie, who'd known her since she was a little girl, jerked his head in Xander's direction and grinned. 'He's good, isn't he?'

'Is there something else I should have said?' Xander asked, bemused.

Having used this exchange to line up her shot, she pressed the clasp on her bag and took a picture. 'You'll take two?' she suggested. 'Along with some chillies, garlic and a handful of those green beans.'

'Some? Is that one of those weird old-fashioned British measurements? Like chains and furlongs?'

'Just ask the man, Xander. He'll know what you mean.'

He turned to the trader. 'I'll take two, Charlie,' he said. 'And some chillies and garlic. And a handful of green beans.'

'Would that be a big handful or a small handful?' Charlie asked.

'Small,' Laura interjected, snorting with laughter.

'And some of those strawberries,' Xander continued, leaving the script and improvising.

'Some?' the trader asked, grinning. 'Only chillies and garlic come in "some".'

'Make me an offer I can't refuse, Charlie.'

They haggled good-naturedly for a minute or two before Charlie took the banknote Xander proffered and said, 'Take your boyfriend away before he ruins me.'

'He's an economist, Charlie.'

'Is that a fact?' He gave Xander his change and the basket. 'We could do with him running the government.' And as he turned away to deal with another customer Xander gave her a look that said, Did I do well?

'I didn't expect you to pay,' she said, not sure whether to be pleased or annoyed at how easily he handled himself in her world. If she'd hoped to make him look foolish she'd failed. 'In fact, I didn't think royalty carried cash.'

'You have deprived me of my normal back-up system, Laura. Even in my ivory tower I am aware that taxi drivers, restaurants, market traders expect to be paid for their services on delivery rather than by account, at the end of the month.'

'How does it feel?'

'So far, so good. Ordinary could get to grow on me.'

'You haven't been on a bus yet.'

'Is that what you've planned for tomorrow?'

Tomorrow? He really was going to do this again tomorrow? He'd said a week, but surely he hadn't meant to spend the entire week with her? 'I haven't thought about tomorrow,' she said. 'Can we go out of London? I mean, do you have to let people know where you are? What about your security people?'

'They tend to panic if I disappear off the face of the earth for more than a couple of hours. Right now they believe I have taken to my bed with a raging fever.'

'It must make—' She was going to say that it must make dating difficult. It seemed intrusive.

But no more intrusive than taking covert photographs. She was a journalist. Asking intrusive questions came with the territory.

'It must make dating difficult,' she said.

'Must it?'

Then, 'How do princes date?'

'Like this?' he offered. Then, while she was still struggling to come to terms with the idea that this was something as simple—or as complex—as a date, 'Where next?'

She gathered her wits and dug an old envelope out of her pocket, suspecting that her leg was being royally pulled.

'I need chicken, fresh basil, some of those tiny pea aubergines from the specialist stall at the other end of the market. Spices. A can of coconut milk,' she said, consulting her list.

'Don't forget some clotted cream for the strawberries,' he said.

'You've ruined my plans for pudding,' she grumbled. 'I was going to poach the peaches in white wine.'

'They'll keep until tomorrow. The strawberries won't.'

'No. Are you absolutely wedded to the idea of clotted cream?' She pulled a face. 'I've got ice cream at home. It's better after curry.'

'We could spoil ourselves and have both,' he suggested. 'That is allowed? In the ordinary world?'

He was laughing at her. Not openly, but the telltale creases at the corners of his eyes betrayed him. How could she have ever thought him haughty? Or arrogant?

She grinned back. 'It's not only allowed, I believe it should be compulsory. Especially if the ice cream is vanilla praline. But I'm afraid we're going to be sick if we try to eat all those strawberries.'

'Not at all. The secret,' he said, his voice softer than a summer mist, 'as in all good things, is to take your time.'

And, just for a moment, she thought she knew exactly what *he* was thinking. Which had to be the purest figment of her imagination.

Her body didn't think so, though. It purred as if stroked and, as he put his hand to her back to steer her through the slow moving traffic, the heat of it seemed to burn through the linen of her shirt, through the T-shirt she was wearing beneath it, right down to her skin.

CHAPTER SIX

ALEXANDER felt like a man let out of chains.

His life was governed by protocol, rules. He knew there was nothing he could do that would not be whispered over, discussed and dissected at length. It had become second nature to him to guard his words, conceal his thoughts and reserve his smile, particularly in the presence of young women, if he wished to avoid the sideways glances, the speculation.

Here no one knew him. No one was interested in the way he looked at Laura, beyond a certain indulgent good humour. Glad to see her happy. Which suggested she hadn't always been so.

Anonymous, he could talk to strangers without the usual constraints, shop for the simple staples of life and carry Laura's basket for her without eyebrows being raised.

Even the simple act of putting his hand on her back as he eased her through the crowds, the traffic, was nothing to be remarked upon, noted as exceptional, apart from a certain lightness in his own heart.

But only he knew about that.

Here, he was no one, and he could drop the mask for a while. Laura was the person everyone was happy to see. They responded to her warmth, as he had done, calling out to her as they toured the market stalls and the local shops and she picked out the food that she was going to cook for them both.

Correction. They were going to cook. Together.

She was wrong about this being ordinary. For him it was far from ordinary. 'Together' was a word that had not featured in his vocabulary in a very long time.

'I'll buy wine for this feast,' he said, as they approached a small specialist shop he'd noticed from the other side of the market.

'No need. Not now we've got the strawberries,' she said, and kept going as if that was an end of it.

He hooked his arm through hers and swung her around.

'Hey!' Her exclamation was cut off as she came to a halt, off balance, with her nose an inch from his chest, grabbing for his shirt-front to steady herself. As he caught her around the waist. Holding her there.

She opened her mouth as if to protest before looking up, and instead caught that beautiful bottom lip between her teeth.

Standing so close to her, her cheeks slightly flushed as she realised that she wasn't talking to the actor who lived upstairs, or some boyfriend she could lead around by the nose, left him feeling much the same.

Speechless.

This morning he'd been at pains to explain to Katie that kissing was something to be saved for the private moments. Right now he understood exactly how she'd felt when she put her arms around that boy's neck and kissed him for the whole world to see. Wanted the whole world to see. Just to show them how happy she was.

'I said,' he said, 'that I will buy wine. Not for poaching peaches but to drink.'

'I'm sorry—'

'No.' He didn't want her to apologise. He loved the fact that she didn't think before she spoke. 'Please. I don't want you to be sorry. I'm having a good time. This is the perfect holiday from real life.'

'This *is* real life, Xander.'

'Not for me.' And he detached one of her hands from his shirt, kissed the back of her fingers. 'I could not do that in real life. At least, not in my real life.'

'N—no,' she managed as the flush to her cheeks deepened, the blue of her eyes almost disappearing as they darkened in response to a gesture that had been anything but courtly. And he had to make a conscious effort to take a step back, put some cool air between them before his own response became an embarrassment to both of them.

'You agree? How refreshing,' he said. 'So, you chose the food; I get to choose what we drink with it. That is fair.'

'It's not—' she began, in a spirited attempt to wrest back control. But her voice caught in her throat. She cleared it, began again. 'It's got nothing to do with fairness. It's just old-fashioned *macho* pride,' she said. 'Food is women's work, but wine—' and she made quotation marks with her fingers '—is a "man" thing.'

'I'm just trying to get some equality going here,' he replied, enjoying himself. He'd forgotten what it felt like to talk so freely.

'You're a fine one to talk about equality when…'

'When what?' he insisted.

'Nothing.' She lifted her hands in a gesture of surrender. 'Sorry, I tend to get a bit carried away. Forget myself.'

'It appears to be catching.' The blush deepened. She kept her eyes firmly cast down, curtained by her lashes. He hooked his fingers beneath her chin and forced her to look up at him. She caught her lower lip nervously between her teeth.

He wanted to do that.

Tug at the soft, inviting flesh. Taste it with his tongue. Taste all of her.

'You're wrong. This has nothing to do with masculine pride. I'm simply playing to my strengths, ma'am.' And he kissed her cheek lightly before, reluctantly, releasing her. 'I may not know much about vegetables, but I do have a vineyard.'

'You do?'

'My one indulgence.' She'd thought he didn't know about being ordinary. She was wrong. He knew… 'And occasionally, if I'm fortunate, for a few weeks a year I can escape to help bring in the harvest.'

For a moment she digested this unexpected revelation. Then she said, 'I bow to your superior knowledge about wine, Xander, but it's traditional to drink beer with a curry,' she said, her voice suddenly less certain, thicker, as if she was having to force the words out. Keep it normal. 'And I have beer at home in the fridge.'

It didn't actually help much, knowing that she was on the same wavelength. Feeling the same way.

Maybe there was something to be said, after all, for kissing in the street. Doing it in public kept things from getting out of hand.

'You don't have to tell me about tradition. I have a thousand years of it to live up to. And I might be new to this, but I'm pretty sure that in the ordinary world it's still traditional that, if the woman cooks, the man brings a bottle.'

'In this case, a bottle of beer. The spices will kill wine stone-dead.'

'You do not give up,' he said. She was stubborn as a mule, but he liked that. He liked that a lot. 'Very well, I surrender to your experience. Beer it is. For the curry. But what are we to do about the strawberries? Trust me, I know about these things. For strawberries you need champagne.'

She sighed. 'You're not playing this by the rules, Xander,' she said, with a more-in-sorrow-than-anger shake of her head. But she could not restrain a smile that lifted his heart even as it lifted the corners of her lovely mouth. 'Champagne is by no means ordinary.'

'No? And in this real world of yours it is not permitted for a man to indulge a woman he likes?' More than likes. Desires.

And his own mouth, with a mind of its own, smiled right back at her.

For a moment she floundered, as if the thought of him actually liking her was difficult to cope with. Then she pulled herself together and said, with mock severity, 'Very well. Just this once. Tomorrow—'

She stopped, blushing fiercely, as if suddenly conscious of going too far. Stepping out of line.

He hated that. Other people did that. He wanted her to feel she could say anything.

'Tomorrow?' he encouraged. 'Have you decided what we're going to do tomorrow?'

She hesitated, a frown buckling her smooth forehead. 'What would you like to do, Xander?'

Spend the day with her. Doing nothing—everything. 'This is your world, Laura. I'm entirely in your hands.' And because the idea of surrendering himself to her was at once exhilarating and unnerving, he turned abruptly away and pushed open the door of the wine shop. 'In all things but champagne.'

Laura, for whom a few pounds spent on a bottle of plonk was an occasional treat, watched while Xander talked knowledgeably about vintages with the owner of the shop before settling on a bottle that, even by champagne prices, was undoubtedly anything but 'ordinary'.

Not that it was a hardship. Watching him. Listening to him. Maybe that was why she completely forgot about taking photographs. Or maybe it was just the lingering throb of her body's response to his touch that was distracting her. Coupled with an uneasy feeling that whatever happened in the next few days, no matter how her career took off as a result of her 'scoop', nothing in her life would ever again be this special.

The first thing Laura saw as she walked through her front door was the red light flashing on the answering machine and her heart sank like a stone. It had to be Trevor McCarthy.

She hadn't phoned him back after he'd sent the camera, unwilling to be grilled about what she knew, what she could deliver. But now he had a photograph of Princess Katerina leaving her flat and would be champing at the bit, eager to find out what was going on.

It could have been worse, she told herself. He could

have called round in person. He already knew she had some connection with the Princess, so that wasn't a real problem. She could tell him the truth about Katie's visit, omitting to mention that her uncle had called, too. But her blood ran cold at the thought of him running into Xander. At the moment he was indulging her, giving her the opportunity to demonstrate just how useless she was so that he could be rid of her once and for all.

But if he knew that Prince Alexander of Montorino had paid her a personal visit he wouldn't risk her messing up the story. He'd put someone else on to it; one photograph would be all that was needed. He could rely on innuendo to do the rest and sell newspapers by the million.

And she'd lose any chance of seeing Xander again.

'I'll take these through to the kitchen, shall I?'

'Sorry?'

'If you want to check your messages?' Xander's expression hadn't changed much. He was still smiling. But she already knew him well enough to distinguish the real thing from the mask.

'It'll probably just be a double glazing salesman with no one to sell to,' she said.

Well, she could hope, couldn't she?

Even from the kitchen he couldn't possibly miss the booming tones of her ex-boss demanding to know what she'd got on His Serene Highness Prince etc, etc.

'Or the pizzeria hoping I can work tonight. Or Sean wanting to borrow my curling tongs.' She frowned. It was a lot easier to frown than sustain that jaunty smile. 'No, wait, he's already got those.'

If she'd hoped that would make him laugh she'd have been disappointed.

'Or it might be something important,' he said, taking the champagne from the basket. 'I'll put this in your fridge.'

And with that he went into the kitchen and closed the door so that she could deal with her calls in privacy. Great. He couldn't have made it plainer that he knew she didn't want him listening in, but then her face had always been an open book. That was why people took advantage of her good nature.

If she was going to stay in this business, she'd have to do some work on her own mask, on hiding her feelings.

She took a deep breath, crossed to the machine. One message. She crossed her fingers and hit 'play'.

It was Jay. 'Darling, that man you did some work for recently called round while you were out. He's wondering if you're going to be able to do anything for him in the near future.'

She smiled in relief. Jay's natural caution with answering machines was legendary. You never knew who might overhear your message, she said. Bless her.

Xander dropped the basket on the kitchen table. Stowed the champagne in the fridge. Tried not to think about the flashing light on Laura's telephone. The way the colour had left her face when she saw it. Tried not to care who was that important in her life.

He had no business caring. No right. He shouldn't even be here. Feeling like this.

He wasn't into fooling himself, but this time he appeared to have managed it wholesale. He'd thought…

No, scrub that. He hadn't been thinking. He hadn't been thinking from the moment he'd walked into the porter's room and Laura Varndell had turned her big blue eyes on him.

Since he'd felt the peachy softness of her skin beneath his fingers.

His imagination would keep taking him on sensory re-run, tempting him to do it again. Take it further. Discover exactly how her mouth would feel beneath his.

He began to empty the basket—anything to keep his mind from drifting to the murmur of her voice through the wall. The soft sound of her laughter.

The door opened behind him and he slammed down the shutters on his imagination and carried on emptying the basket.

'Now, that,' Laura said, grinning, 'is domesticated.'

'Not ordinary at all, then,' he said, his own mood deteriorating in direct proportion to her cheerfulness.

'Not in your world, maybe.'

If she'd picked up on his change of mood she wasn't letting it affect hers. Maybe she didn't notice. Maybe her caller had made her too happy to care.

'Would you like some tea?' she asked, stowing the vegetables in the fridge. 'We could sit outside in the garden.'

'How very English,' he said. Feeling suddenly very foreign indeed. Out of his depth. Unimportant. He did not like feeling unimportant, he discovered. Not in

Laura Varndell's life, anyway. 'Will we have cucumber sandwiches and scones?'

'With home-made strawberry preserve?' she asked, amused by this, too, apparently. Her mood was beyond dampening. 'Sorry, this is ordinary life, remember? Not some nostalgic Hollywood version of England. I might have a packet of chocolate biscuits somewhere, though. And you could have coffee if you prefer. Or something cold?'

'What about this curry?' he said, hell-bent on irritating her. 'Don't we have to start chopping onions?'

'Not instantly,' she said. 'It doesn't take long to cook.' Then, finally responding to his tone, she shut the fridge door and turned to face him. 'Unless you've got a curfew? Will your minions raise the alarm, call out the guard, if you don't return before dark?'

He refused to make it that easy for her. 'If you'd prefer me to leave early, just say.'

Laura had realised the minute she'd entered the kitchen that Xander had reverted to distant autocrat. Was he really offended that she'd given her attention to her unknown caller? Or just offended that she'd *had* a caller when she was supposed to be giving him her undivided attention? And in a moment her mood had switched from guilt to anger.

He might be king of the castle where he came from, but this was her home. Her life.

'That,' she said, lobbing the ball straight back into his court, 'is entirely up to you.'

He shrugged. 'It occurs to me that you weren't expecting me to stay all evening,' he said, not answering her question. But then, she'd not answered his.

'Maybe you have other plans? A previous commitment?'

Commitment. Nice word. Covered all eventualities. 'Do you mean a date?' she asked. 'I did invite you to stay, Xander.'

'That's generous of you, but I believe I invited myself. I forget sometimes that people assume my simplest thought, spoken out loud, is an order.'

'Not me. If I'd had a date, I'd have told you so.'

'If you've put someone off—' He left the sentence hanging, leaving her to fill in the blank.

So. He'd heard her talking to Jay and instantly assumed that she was breaking some poor sap's heart on his account. How arrogant could one man get? He didn't deserve to be put out of his misery. But she wanted to put that smile back on his face.

'The message on the machine was from my aunt, Xander. Someone called for me, wanting to talk about a job.'

'Now?' He let slip the aristocratic pose. 'Don't let me—'

'I won't! Now, for goodness' sake, if you don't want tea, take a beer and go and sit outside in the sun. Relax.'

'What about Sean?' he persisted.

'What is this? Twenty questions?'

'Won't he be dropping in for...coffee?'

He wasn't suspicious, or on his aristocratic high horse, she realised, belatedly. He was just plain jealous.

This man, this prince who had a whole country at his feet, who could snap his fingers and have his pick of the beauties of Montorino—or anywhere else for that matter—was jealous of her narcissistic neighbour.

She didn't know whether to be cross with him, laugh at him, or hug him. She did none of those things, too touched, moved, by this unexpected evidence of self-doubt. Uncertainty.

It was so…human.

So ordinary.

'Sean's got a walk-on part as a spear-carrier at the National this season. He won't be home until very late.'

It was unkind not to be totally reassuring. But he wasn't the only one needing a little reassurance here. Xander had come within a whisper's breath of kissing her back there, outside the wine shop. Really kissing her. And she'd come within a whisper's breath of letting him.

'How late?' he demanded. Reassuringly.

'Early or late makes no difference, Xander. Coffee is all he'd ever get from me.'

'You're not…?' She didn't answer, merely raised her eyebrows as if she didn't understand what he was asking. Forcing him to be explicit. 'You and Sean?'

A little short on content, perhaps, but the meaning was unmistakable. He wanted to know if they were lovers.

'I don't date my tenants, Xander. Not even the good-looking ones.' And she took a beer out of the fridge and put it in his hand. 'Outside, now, while I put this stuff away.'

She joined him in her tiny garden. He was stretched out on one of the huge old-fashioned bamboo recliners that Jay had brought back from somewhere in the Far East, eyes closed, feet up, a tiny give away smile suggesting that he was well pleased with life.

'This is good,' he said. 'I could get used to ordinary.'

'If the peasants revolt you won't be too unhappy, then?'

'My people are not peasants,' he said sharply, not as sleepy as he looked.

'It was simply an expression, Xander.'

'I know. Even so. They are highly educated, forward-thinking—'

'They are disenfranchised.'

'You think so?' That appeared to amuse him. 'Montorinans are mountain people. No one can make them do anything against their will. They have their own way of making their feelings known. Local councils to speak for their communities. But, all appearances to the contrary, I'm a benevolent tyrant. I don't even beat the servants, despite the way that silly girl behaved yesterday.'

'No?' she asked, as if she needed convincing.

'It appears that it was her first day and she was nervous. I spoke to her this morning. Made sure to wear my best smile in an effort to reassure her that she wasn't about to become an unemployment statistic. Please don't tell anyone about that.' His expression remained deadpan. 'It'll be bad for my image. I'm supposed to be autocratic and unfeeling.'

'You look the part,' she assured him. 'I have to tell you, as a neutral observer—' neutral? '—that you've failed the practical. You are, however, living in the past.'

'When you're dealing with a thousand years of tradition, change is slow. And my grandfather is an old man. Fixed in his ways.'

Oh, right. So she'd been wrong about that, too. 'You'll make changes when...' Her turn to stop and consider what she was saying.

'When he dies and I become head of state in name as well as reality?' he completed for her. She got a re-run of his wry smile. 'You see my problem. It's not like a boardroom coup where the loser just gets to spend more time working on his golf handicap. Retirement from this job is final.'

'Tell me about Montorino,' she encouraged. 'I've seen photographs in the travel supplements and it looks beautiful.'

'It is beautiful, Laura. Mountains, vineyards, lakes. Peaceful villages. Even the capital city looks like something out of a fairy story.'

'But behind the medieval architecture is a modern banking industry.'

'Bankers like peace.' He shrugged. 'There's something to be said for being off the beaten track of history. If we'd been strategically important we'd have been overrun centuries ago.'

'It sounds heavenly.'

'No, this is heaven.'

She surveyed her little garden. The early roses were scenting the air, and the vivid plantings of petunias and impatiens were practically bursting out of their pots.

'The slugs certainly think so,' she said, lying back on the other recliner.

If she was honest with herself, this wasn't exactly

what she'd had in mind when she proposed His Highness try a taste of life without the princely trappings. She'd been hoping he'd suffer, just a little.

But what the heck. She closed her eyes. There was no rush.

The onions could wait.

Xander watched her for a while, marvelling at the way she had just closed her eyes and fallen asleep almost in the same instant.

Who was she, this girl who'd erupted into his life? Karl, the only person who knew where he was today—even when he was suspending his own life for an hour or two someone had to know where he was in case of an emergency—had earned his unwarranted wrath for raising doubt. Urging caution.

He did not want to doubt her. He wanted to throw caution to the wind and let down his guard, responding to that reflection of his own loneliness that he saw in her. Something that urged him to reach out to her. Take her hand with a reckless disregard for the consequences.

But why should she be lonely? She was lovely, full of life. Refreshingly full of opinions that she was happy to share with him, whether he wanted to hear them or not. A joyful woman, to whom any man would gladly give his heart.

So, bearing all that in mind, maybe it was time to ask himself exactly what she had been doing outside his house last night. Where had she been going?

It was as if he had suspended all his critical faculties from the moment he set eyes on Laura Varndell.

As if his well-honed instinct for self-preservation had deserted him.

Or maybe he had simply wanted to believe that she was exactly what she said she was. A public-spirited citizen who happened to be passing at the critical moment.

As Katie would say, How likely was that?

This was his opportunity to find out.

He left her sleeping in the garden and went into her sitting room. It was small but welcoming, the dark polished floor covered with an old tribal rug. Small, precious curios from distant places were tucked away on shelves. There was a cream linen-covered sofa. A saggy armchair. Book-lined walls. He scanned the titles. Travel, biographies, mountaineering. An odd interest for someone afraid of heights. But then her father had been a mountaineer, she'd said.

Varndell wasn't a common name. It should be easy enough to check.

Even as he thought it he saw a little row of books with the name Bruce Varndell on the spines. The photograph of a fair, open-faced man on the back dispelled any doubt. The family likeness was clear enough. He slid it back into place, feeling dangerously light-hearted. And he continued to look around.

Only a copy of *Celebrity* magazine, the one with his photograph on the cover, which had slipped down behind the small writing table in the window, seemed out of place.

Jarred.

Suggested that he was right to doubt that her fortuitous appearance last night had been pure chance.

He picked it up, placed it next to her shoulder bag,

abandoned on the table when she'd listened to her messages. It was an old bag, well used, undoubtedly a favourite or it would have been long abandoned.

His hand paused briefly over the leather, but he couldn't bring himself to open it and instead moved on to the telephone with its built-in answering machine. The answering machine had been turned off. Well, that was to be expected since she was home. But the telephone had been unplugged from its socket. Which was not.

It was time, then, for a reality check and he plugged in the phone, lifted the receiver and hit 'redial' before he could think of some excuse not to.

The phone rang twice before it was picked up and a clear, bright voice said, 'Jay Varndell.'

He replaced the receiver, unplugged the phone and went back out into the garden to watch the gentle rise and fall of Laura's quiet breathing as she slept.

Wishing, with all his heart, he hadn't done that, but instead trust to his own instincts.

CHAPTER SEVEN

LAURA woke with a start. The sun had dipped behind the houses so that her garden was in shade and she shivered a little as she sat up, stretching and yawning widely. Then nearly broke her jaw trying to snap her mouth shut as, too late, she saw Xander watching her.

She groaned. 'I'm so sorry! How long have I been asleep?' Then she groaned again. 'Please tell me I didn't snore,' she begged.

'You didn't snore,' he said, but with the kind of grin that cancelled out any possibility of reassurance.

Forget snoring. Had she talked in her sleep? She'd used to do that when she was disturbed, and Xander Orsino was the most disturbing man she'd ever met.

'And don't apologise. You must have been tired,' Xander said. 'You had a late night, courtesy of Katie. You really shouldn't have stayed up worrying about her.'

'No, I shouldn't.' She should have turned in her story and gone to bed like any sensible journalist. But then, according to Trevor, 'sensible' and 'journalist' were not words he'd ever use to describe her. 'She's clearly more than capable of looking after herself.'

'I wouldn't go as far as that. But she did have her minder keeping an eye on her.'

'I know, but I felt responsible. For letting her fool me. I'm just so gullible.'

'Don't be so hard on yourself.'

'No, really, it's true. I was at this rock festival once when a girl asked me to hold her baby while she went to the loo. I didn't see her again for two days.'

'Let me guess. You did not immediately hand the baby over to the Social Services.'

'I couldn't do that! They might have taken her into care. The poor girl just needed a break. She'd left her bag. With the nappies and formula and everything.' She shrugged. 'Of course I didn't see much of the festival.' She hadn't seen much of anything. Babies, she'd discovered, were a full-time job. Which, since she'd been sent, as the youngest member of the team, to report on the festival scene, wasn't good.

'If anyone else had told me that story,' Xander said, getting to his feet, 'I might have doubted it.'

'But you've had first-hand experience of just how gullible I can be.'

'You are kind, Laura. Thoughtful. Caring. And I have no doubt that faced with a similar situation you'd act in exactly the same way.'

'I'm not sure whether to be flattered or insulted.'

'No?' His brows kinked upwards as he extended a hand to help her to her feet. 'I thought my meaning was clear enough.'

'I'm a fool?' she offered, taking his hand. He didn't step back as she got up and she wobbled uncertainly in an attempt not to crash into him. He looped his arm around her waist to steady her. Hold her close. 'But a kind fool.' And to prove it, she lifted herself up on her toes to kiss his cheek before disengaging his hand from her waist and, keeping it firmly in hers, she headed for the kitchen. 'Come along, Your Highness. It's time to demonstrate that I'm not a total pushover.'

'You're wishing you'd never agreed to this, aren't you?' Laura said, tugging on her lower lip as she tried hard not to laugh.

'No, really.' Xander continued to slice onions, promising himself never to take the humble vegetable for granted again. He lifted his hand to wipe away the tears, but she reached out and grabbed it before he could. And for a moment neither of them felt like laughing.

Then she dropped his hand, turned quickly away. 'You'll get the juice in your eyes and then you'll really have something to cry about.' She opened her bag, which had somehow migrated from the living room, found a clean handkerchief and reached up, leaning into him as she blotted his cheeks with the lightest touch.

He caught her at the waist to steady her, his fingers flaring out over her hips. In that moment he would have given anything to be just an ordinary man—not just for a week, but for the rest of his life—so that he could bury his face in her soft, sweet-smelling hair, warm from the sun.

'You'd better chop the beans and leave the chillies to me before you do yourself some real mischief,' she said, pulling back, rescuing him from a temptation that had been shockingly real. Not quite meeting his eyes. 'There, is that better?'

For a moment he considered saying no. Insist she do the decent thing and kiss him better. Reprise the rush of hot desire that had flooded through him as she'd kissed his cheek. Reprise the sheer pleasure of watching her blush scarlet again, at her own boldness.

When he didn't immediately answer she lifted her lashes, met his gaze head on, and he got a lot more than he'd bargained for. A thousand-megawatt jolt from the arc lamps of her eyes, jump-starting his heart as well as his body.

Still feeling guilty for spying on her, he made a valiant effort at self-restraint.

'Don't let the tears fool you. I can handle a few chillies,' he said. He picked up the knife, used it to push away the pile of onions. 'How difficult can it be?'

'It isn't. Just make sure you don't wipe your eyes afterwards, okay? Or put your hands near your mouth. Or anything else...sensitive.' And she blushed anyway, rousing an answering heat in his own weak flesh. He wanted her in a way that left him helpless, floundering.

'Sensitive?' His throat felt as if it were stuffed with glue.

'You have the future of the house of Orsino to consider.'

'Ah,' he said.

But it wasn't the risk of burning delicate flesh that had dealt with his simmering libido.

Grinning, she passed him the beans, then, pausing only to shift her bag out of the way, set about de-seeding the chillies.

'Isn't it about time you started thinking about that?'

He glanced up, but she was concentrating on what she was doing. 'Thinking about what?'

'The future of the house of Orsino. Isn't it your

duty to produce an heir and a spare?' Realising that he had stopped chopping the beans, she looked up. 'There were rumours, about eight years ago. Speculation about a girl you'd met at university. Juliet—?'

'You have done your homework.'

'I have the latest issue of *Celebrity*,' she admitted. 'She was described as the girl who broke your heart.'

'Is that right?'

'They said that you've never looked seriously at another woman.' She became self-conscious, as if aware she'd stepped over some unseen line into forbidden territory. Concentrated on the chillies. 'I'm sorry. I'm being intrusive. I told you that I have this mouth that gets me into trouble all the time.'

'Not at all. My life is an open book, as you have just demonstrated. Everything I do is news. Any woman I look at more than once. I hope you're prepared for that.'

'Me?' she squeaked, her eyes widening in alarm as she abandoned her task.

'After Ascot your name will also be linked with mine in every article, in every newspaper or magazine, until the end of time. And with about as much accuracy.'

'Oh. Oh, I see.' She lifted her shoulders, embarrassed that she'd fallen for journalistic creativity. 'Did she mind?'

'She laughed it off at the time, but I imagine it irritates the hell out of her husband now she's married.'

'Why? Even if she had been the love of your life, she still chose him.'

'Hey, I'm the pragmatic one, remember?'

'It must be catching. I'm prepared for the reaction of the press. I'll cope.'

'If I had doubted it, I would not have involved you. I wonder, even for Katie, whether I should do this. If you have any real idea of the pressure....'

'Is that what happened?' she asked. 'With Juliet?'

'Juliet was a friend, nothing more. I stayed with her family in Norfolk after my grandmother died and I needed a quiet place to think. Be alone.' He attacked the beans with his knife. 'Not much chance of that once the press found out I was there. Believe me, Laura, if I loved any woman enough to ask her to share my life, I would love her enough to walk away. Spare her that.' He looked up, met her gaze head-on. 'Does that answer your question? About an heir?'

'I'm so sorry, Xander.'

Obviously it did. She had not needed his meaning spelled out in words of one syllable. Had understood that in rejecting marriage he was also sacrificing the joy of fatherhood.

'Don't be. It's not your fault.'

But her eyes had filled up and he reached out, covered her hand with his, held it for a moment.

She blinked. 'It's just the beastly onions,' she said, brushing a tear from her cheek with the back of her wrist.

'You're right about champagne and strawberries,' Laura said, light-headed and replete. 'A winning combination.'

'And you were right about the ice-cream. The curry was good, too.' Xander glanced at the pile of dishes on the draining board. 'I guess this is the point in the proceedings where you instruct me in the noble art of washing up.'

'That was the plan,' she admitted, 'but I've decided to let you off and own up to the dishwasher.'

'I have to admit that I stumbled across it when I was looking for a pan. But I wasn't going to spoil your fun.'

'Really? You've been very sporting. Of course I wouldn't stop you if you insisted on stacking it. The dishwasher.'

'I insist,' he said gamely.

It was extraordinary, she thought, watching him scrape dishes, load the machine. Yesterday he had seemed as distant as the stars. This evening she was totally at ease with him. Far from being the cold, arrogant prince that his photographs suggested, he was intelligent, stimulating, amusing.

They'd laughed over the same things, discovered a shared love of twentieth-century art, modern jazz, sailing, found themselves finishing each other's half-spoken thoughts.

'You're not making a bad job of that,' she said, feeling just a touch light-headed.

'For a man?'

'For a prince. I don't imagine you've done it before.'

'No, but it is simply a question of applying logic—' which seemed screamingly funny for some reason '—and order to the task.' She exploded into a fit of giggles. He closed the dishwasher door, looked at the settings, chose one that appeared appropriate and then switched it on. Which was even funnier. 'I'm afraid the champagne has gone to your head,' he said, turning to look at her.

'No, honestly.' It was the fact that he hadn't put any detergent in the machine that was so funny. She made an effort to be serious. 'It wasn't the champagne. It was the strawberries.'

'Of course, how silly of me,' he said, humouring her. Before she could get cross, he said, 'Shall I make some coffee?'

He picked up the kettle, but she got up, took it from him. 'My turn. Go through to the sitting room, put your feet up.'

But instead he stayed where he was, leaning back against the kitchen table. Watching her.

'Thank you for a lovely day, Laura. If this is ordinary life, I could get used to it.'

'Don't be too hasty. I'm sure the novelty will wear off very quickly.'

'While I am certain that Ladies' Day will come far too soon. What time shall I pick you up in the morning? About ten?'

At which point she stopped wanting to laugh. She didn't want him to pick her up in the morning. She wanted him to stay....

'Ten?' No. Yes. 'Great,' she said unenthusiastically.

'If that's inconvenient, please say. I do not wish to take your hospitality for granted.'

'Of course it's not *inconvenient*,' she declared. 'Will you please just stop being so damned considerate for a minute and let me think?' Her hand flew to her mouth. 'I'm so sorry.'

He took hold of her wrist, pulled her hand away

and kissed her. No ceremony. No long lingering look. None of that shall-we shan't-we tango. Just a swift, hard kiss that lasted not nearly long enough considering the aftershock that exploded through her body like a blast wave.

'Why did you do that?' she demanded, probably because her brain was no longer functioning in any meaningful fashion.

'To stop you from saying that wretched word. To stop you from leaping to apologise every time you say the first thing that comes into your head. Consider it a fixed penalty,' he said, suddenly angry with her. Angry with himself. 'Any objections?'

'Er, no,' she said. Not one she could think of.

His expression softened. 'And because—if you insist upon the truth—I wanted to kiss you very badly.'

'Then you failed,' she said, delighting in the slightly puzzled frown that buckled the space between his brows. 'You don't kiss badly at all.' Then, 'Sorry…' she began, but this time not entirely without thought. Testing his resolve. He laid a warning finger briefly against her lips. Too clever by half. 'Very bad schoolgirl-type joke.'

'Tell me what's bothering you about tomorrow, Laura.'

Oh, well. She mustn't be greedy. She hauled her brain back into action and turned away, pushing the spout of the kettle beneath the tap to fill it. 'It's just that I don't think it's such a great idea, you coming here.' Not with Trevor on the prowl. 'That photographer could be hanging around.'

'Why should he be doing that?'

'They've seen Katie visit me. They don't give up,

you said, and you should know. You're the one who's put his life into cold storage.'

Maybe it was just as well that the kettle chose that moment to overflow, the water gushing up the spout and spurting everywhere. She leapt back as the cold water hit her square in the face, the chest, dropping the kettle in the sink. This didn't help. The water sprayed up off the domed lid of the kettle and continued to shower her and the kitchen until Xander braved the deluge to turn it off.

'I've been complaining about the water pressure for months,' she gasped, trying to get her breath back, tugging the freezing sodden shirt from her skin. 'They appear to have finally done something about it.' And only then did she turn to survey the damage.

Actually, the kitchen wasn't as bad as she'd expected. Most of the water had got her. The remainder appeared to be dripping from Xander.

He'd already unbuttoned his shirt, was tugging it out of his jeans. And as he peeled it off she forgot all about her soaking. The wet linen clinging to her skin. Dripping hair.

'Have you got a towel?' he prompted, after a moment during which she could not tear her gaze from his golden-skinned shoulders, a chest which—if she had ever fantasised about such things—would comply with the most demanding specification.

'What? Towel?' She blinked, blanking out the image and managing to regain control of her wits. 'Oh, good grief! What am I thinking?'

She raced through her bedroom into her tiny *en suite* bathroom before he could answer that, flinging open the cupboard and grabbing the first two towels that came to hand.

She got as far as the door before she tossed them aside and turned back for some new ones she'd been saving for best.

How much better could it get?

She turned to find him behind her. 'Sorry I was so long.' He forestalled her apology, taking the towels from her, draping one over her dripping hair, wrapping it up turban-style. 'That was for you.'

'I'm fine. I've hung my shirt outside. It'll be dry in a few minutes. You're the one soaked through.'

'Am I?' she asked stupidly. Of course she was. 'Well, that doesn't matter,' she said. 'This is England. We're used to getting wet, while you're used to— What are you *doing*?'

Totally stupid question. What he was doing was plainly obvious, even to her. He was unbuttoning her shirt. Correction, he'd unbuttoned her shirt—memo to brain: must get shirts with more buttons. Give herself more time to get her brain into gear, her mouth into action.

'Xander—'

She might as well have saved her breath. He ignored her warning with princely arrogance and her skin goosed as he peeled the cold wet cloth from her skin and tossed it into the tub.

Just as well it was a black vest top she was wearing beneath it. If it had been white he'd have been able to see straight through it.

Unfortunately, nothing could disguise the way her nipples were standing out like a pair of doorstops. She just hoped he hadn't cottoned on to the fact that this had absolutely nothing to do with the cold. Or the wet.

He unravelled the turban and began to dry the ends of her hair. On the point of telling him that there was no need, that she was perfectly capable of drying her own hair, she managed to curb her overactive tongue.

He was doing a fine job.

He transferred his attention to her neck.

Absolutely great.

Then he brushed aside the straps of the top and turned his attention to her shoulders. And suddenly speech was not something she was willing to attempt. Besides, what would she say? Stop?

Okay, so she should say that. But his hand, warm beneath the towel, seemed to have turned on some central heating system inside her and, as he brushed the soft, fluffy towel across her throat, mopping up the drips trickling into her cleavage before working towards her other shoulder, the boiler was going full blast.

She didn't want to do, or say, one thing that would switch it off.

Apparently satisfied that her shoulders were thoroughly dry, he pulled her against him and began to dry her back. Was her back wet? Surely not. Did she care? Not one jot. And her mouth, far from calling a halt, simply curved into a contented little smile as she lay her cheek against his chest.

His body was solid, safe, in contrast to the yielding languor of her feeble limbs. She could feel the ripple of muscles as he eased up the vest, stroking the towel up her back as he exposed her naked flesh. Feel the slow, powerful thud of his heartbeat.

Hers wasn't slow. It was breaking the speed limit and heading for trouble. Too late now to wish she'd worn a bra.

Not that she actually did. Wish that.

He abandoned the towel in favour of his hands and she shivered with pleasure as they encompassed her waist and moved, slow, unimpeded, over her back beneath her damp vest.

'Arms up,' he said thickly.

Her limbs were boneless, her mind out to lunch as he eased the damp garment over her head, let it drop to the floor.

She should move, she thought.

None of her limbs responded and then one of those very capable hands was spread across her back, holding her exactly where she was. Moving now would be rude, she decided, and stopped worrying about it.

With the other, he touched her hair. Stroked it.

Clearly checking that it was dry.

'You have the most beautiful hair,' he said, grazing his lips over it. 'It smells like…fresh air.' He slid his long fingers through it, left them there, cupping her head in his hand, while his mouth lingered momentarily at her temple before he tilted it back, forcing her to look up at him, confront a desire that was already plainly evident.

Too late to move, even if she'd wanted to. She was finding it difficult enough simply to breathe.

'I've been doing my best to avoid temptation, Laura.'

'Have you?' Her words were cobweb-soft, squeezed from a throat that seemed to have no substance.

He had the most beautiful mouth, she thought. Why hadn't she noticed that when she'd been studying all those photographs of him in *Celebrity*? On the internet?

His lower lip was full, sensuous. A wicked enticement to any girl.

'Why?' she asked, feeling utterly, wonderfully, wicked.

Why had she ever thought his eyes cold? They were dark as night—right now they were almost black—but anything but cold. They were glittering with fire and hot enough to scorch her skin.

'There is—' he murmured, the authoritarian ring to his voice blurred out of existence '—a very good reason. But right now I can't remember what it is.'

And then he lowered his lips to hers.

Laura's mouth was hot silk. Honey-sweet. Her pale skin luminous in the dusky half-light of a perfect summer's evening. There were moments that would stay in the heart for ever and as she lifted her arms, wound them around his neck and surrendered to him, Xander knew that this was one of them.

'Laura?'

As he made a final desperate bid to stop this before he did something he knew would cause them both untold pain, she took his lower lip into her mouth, tasted it, sliding her tongue inside his mouth with a soft, sweet moan, stopping the words, silencing his conscience, obliterating everything but this precious moment.

'I'm giving you a week, Xander,' she murmured as she leaned back to look up at him, her eyes hot sapphires. 'A chance to be an ordinary man, just for a little while. Take it. Love me.'

It would take a man of stone to reject her. A heart of ice not to melt in the warmth of such sweet seduction. He had tried, God alone knew, to be both ice and stone, but he was flesh and blood, an ordinary man who was powerless to resist this tender, loving gift of the heart.

She unclasped her hands, slid them over his chest, not looking at him now, but concentrating on unthreading his belt buckle. Slipping the button at his waist.

He captured her hands, stopped her. 'I desired you from the first moment I set eyes on you, Laura,' he said fiercely, wanting her to remember that always. To know that he wasn't simply using her. And then he lifted her hands to his lips and kissed first the knuckles, then the palms, the fingers.

Only then did he sweep her up into his arms, carry her to the huge old-fashioned bed with its hand-pieced quilt that dominated her bedroom as if it had been simply waiting for this night.

Afterwards he held her as she slept, cradling her against his body, watching the quiet rise and fall of her breast until the soft light of dawn crept in across the garden, touching the tangled silvery mass of her hair, warming her skin.

So much for his much-vaunted self-control. A sense of duty that bound him to a destiny that had destroyed the lives of his own parents and which he'd sworn he would never inflict on any child of his.

In the years since he'd made his decision never to

marry there had been no shortage of suitably aristocratic women, beautiful women, trailed past him by his grandfather in an attempt to persuade him to change his mind. No shortage of glamorous women with their hearts set on a title who had made it their personal business to guide him to the altar.

He had not always resisted temptation; he had never pretended he was a saint. But he'd never been less than honest. And not one of them had shaken his conviction that in rejecting marriage he was doing the right thing.

He had believed it was because he was strong. In control of this one aspect of his life. But now he was face to face with the truth. That he'd never before met a woman for whom his sacrifice would have had any real meaning.

Until twenty-four hours ago when Laura Varndell had erupted into his life. Finally, as he looked into a life stretching forty, fifty years into the future, he understood the enormity of his decision.

She shifted, turned, her lips parting a little in what might have been a smile. Happy in her sleep.

He bent to gently kiss the smile, hesitated, unwilling to risk disturbing her. The only reason to wake her would be to say goodbye. To tell her that she had done everything she'd set out to achieve. That for one afternoon, evening, night, she had shown him what it could be to be an ordinary man.

But he wasn't ordinary, and he'd be forced to watch her smile fade as reality seeped back into their lives along with the daylight.

I'm giving you a week, she'd said.

But he couldn't risk a week.

She had melted the ice around his heart with the heat of her love. Battered down the wall of detachment that had protected him from emotional involvement.

Now, when it would hurt—really hurt—he had to walk away. Prove to himself that, when it mattered, he could keep his promise never to risk the happiness of a woman he loved.

As if the pain he was feeling reached out and touched Laura in her sleep, the smooth space between her brows puckered in a frown and she woke, reaching out without hesitation first to touch his face, then to kiss him.

'Thank you,' she murmured.

'What for?'

'Staying. Holding me while I slept. Loving me. For being an ordinary prince as well as an extraordinary one.'

His turn to stop her words. To hold her one last time, possess her and give himself, heart and soul without reservation. To tell her, with his body, all the things that he could not say with words.

CHAPTER EIGHT

'I HAVE to go, Laura.'

'Of course you do,' she said, with absolutely no intention of letting Xander leave her bed in the immediate future. Not until she'd hand-fed him breakfast, anyway. 'Obviously it'll cause a terrific scandal in the servants' hall if the upstairs maid discovers your bed hasn't been slept in.'

'Idiot,' he said, which despite the unflattering sentiment she rather enjoyed, since he accompanied it with a kiss.

Two days ago he would never have said that.

'You mean it's such a common occurrence that it *won't* provoke gossip?'

'I give up. This is a game I can't win.'

'Well, *hello*. I seem to be making headway here.' Not as much as she'd like, though, since he made a determined effort to disentangle himself and swung himself out of bed, reaching for his jeans.

For a moment she watched the ripple of golden, well-honed flesh, then she hauled her brain back into action and said, 'Okay, I'll give you an hour to go and prove to your security people that you aren't being held prisoner in a Notting Hill basement. After that I come and get you.' She grinned. 'You still need work in the ordinary department.'

He wasn't laughing. 'Laura, I have to tell you something.'

She kneeled up, wrapping a sheet around her, not quite liking the serious tone, the hard set of his jaw. 'I'm listening,' she said. Although she had a sudden premonition that she wouldn't like what she was going to hear.

He looked around for his shirt, then remembered that it was outside. She clambered down from the bed and followed him, trailing the sheet, watching him as he buttoned himself into the shirt, reached in his breast pocket, frowning as he checked his pager for messages.

'Xander?'

He glanced at her. Shook his head. 'Not now. Later.'

'Look out for photographers on your way out, won't you?' she said, hating the way he was already shifting away from her, not physically, but inside his head where it really mattered.

'I should be used to them by now,' he said dryly. But, tempted as she was to utter the forbidden word, she decided that on this occasion discretion might be the better part of valour since he didn't look exactly thrilled by her warning.

Or maybe it was the message dragging him back to his own version of ordinary.

'Is something wrong?'

'Karl has been trying to reach me.'

'Call him—he could muss up your bed for you.'

He smiled finally, leaned in to kiss her, hold her for a moment. 'I have to go.'

Of course. Affairs of state beckoned. She reached up, took his face in her hands. 'Okay, Xander. Go deal with whatever crisis demands your personal attention. But don't forget that I have first call on your time for the next week. And—' she continued, her voice the only firm thing about her '—unless you've gone to war overnight, I'll meet you in the kitchenware department in Claibourne & Farraday at twelve o'clock—'

'Claibourne & Farraday? Whatever happened to "ordinary"?'

She lifted her shoulders in the merest shrug. Katie wasn't the only one capable of acting her heart out in a good cause. 'It'll be busy,' she said, banking on the fact that he wanted to talk to her to get him there. She knew he'd stepped way over the line in the sand he'd drawn for himself. She wasn't about to let him step back without putting up a fight. 'And I need a part for my food mixer. Don't speak to me, just follow me when I leave.'

'Very cloak and dagger,' he said.

'Only in the most ordinary way. Don't be late.'

He said nothing, simply reached out, briefly touching her cheek before walking quickly away. She flinched as the front door banged shut behind him.

Ordinary? How could a day spent with Alexander Orsino be ordinary? She touched her cheek, then her lips, still throbbing from his kisses.

How could a day without him ever be anything else?

Laura went back to bed, curling up in the place where Xander had lain, hugging his pillow against her as she relived the past twenty-four hours.

Every look, every touch, every laugh they'd shared.

He'd opened up, told her things that she'd never,

even in her wildest dreams, expected to hear from his lips. His decision never to marry, for instance.

She sensed that it wasn't the whole story, not by a long way, but even as the most useless journalist with an up-to-date press card she knew the value of that piece of information. She could imagine the headlines even as she lay there drowning in the lingering scent of his body. Headlines with her byline.

Not so useless.

She had her story, photographs that would earn her a fortune from *Celebrity* magazine, the European press. She'd been in the right place at the right time and her career was about to lift off into the stratosphere.

Except—what was that worth set against the fact that Xander trusted her? Really trusted her. Had let down every barrier, surrendering himself to her in every way a man could.

And it was then that she recognised a truth about herself. Trevor was right; she would never be a journalist. Not in a million years.

No journalist would even think twice about using what she knew, while there was nothing on earth that would make her surrender the film in her camera to Trevor McCarthy.

She might be a fool, but she was one who knew the value of integrity, truth, honesty. One who was not about to delude herself with fantasies of some happy-ever-after fairy tale, either.

She knew what he was going to say to her.

That this wasn't his real life. That it couldn't last.

As if she hadn't known that when she'd kissed him.

But she'd weep later, when he wasn't around to

see. In the meantime she would give him a week out of her life, offer him a brief moment of happiness. It would be enough to know that she would live in his heart as a true friend.

'Hi, Jay—great timing, you can help me decide what to wear.'

Jay followed Laura into her bedroom and eyed askance the clothes piled up on her bed. 'Where are you going?'

'Out.'

'I think I'm going to need a bit more of a clue.'

'Just out. I haven't decided. Look around some galleries, maybe. Or maybe we'll take a ride into the country.'

'These are elegant,' Jay said, picking up a pair of taupe trousers. 'And I'd wear the cream silk shirt and that linen jacket.' Then, 'We?'

Oh, fig! 'No one you know.' Then, quickly, 'Did you come down for something in particular?'

'Only to ask why you phoned me yesterday. I called back, but got no answer. I knew if it was important you'd come up. But since I was passing—' She lifted her shoulders in the barest suggestion of a shrug.

'You know why I phoned you, Jay. We spoke about Trevor McCarthy.'

'Your second call. About half an hour later? Maybe a little more.'

Laura shook her head. 'It wasn't me. I unplugged the phone right after I talked to you. I didn't want Trevor calling me while Xander was here.'

The name just slipped out.

'Xander? That's short for Alexander, isn't it?' She didn't wait for confirmation. 'I was going to ask how the story's going.'

'But?' Furious at the look of doubt on Jay's face, she said, 'His Serene Highness stayed for supper. In fact, he stayed all night.'

'Oh.' That wasn't a surprised or excited 'oh'. It was one of those flat, oh dear 'oh's that can only mean one thing. Trouble.

'Oh? Is that all you can say?'

'Maybe it's all I should say.'

'And what does that mean? Come on, you'd better tell me.'

'It's just that my phone rang about half an hour or so after I'd spoken to you. I wasn't wearing my specs so I couldn't see the number calling and I answered it with my name, as I always do. Whoever called hung up without speaking and you know how that irritates me, so I fetched my specs to see who it was. The number was yours, Laura.'

Oh, indeed.

And without warning her joyful mood shattered into a million pieces as she realised that Xander had been checking up on her.

She'd dozed off in the sun and he hadn't wasted a second, apparently. Plugging in the phone, pressing 'redial' to find out who she'd called. Just in case she'd been lying to him.

He hadn't been jealous. He'd been suspicious. And the moment she'd closed her eyes he'd done a little checking up. And the first place he'd have looked would have been her handbag.

The camera was neatly hidden from view between

the lining and the leather. She could open it with impunity and no one would ever suspect it was there. But it would never fool anyone with his hand in her bag.

What else was in it? Not her press pass. She'd had the sense to take that out of her wallet. Not that it mattered. A hidden camera was all the evidence he'd need that she was up to no good.

And that was when he'd plugged in her telephone and used the redial button to find out who she'd called.

Then he'd allowed her to think she was getting away with it. No wonder he was in such a good mood. He'd doubtless opened up the back of the camera and exposed the film to the light so that it was useless.

She'd have nothing.

Unlike His Serene Highness Prince Alexander Michael George Orsino. He'd had everything she promised him. Everything he wanted. Even her begging him to make love to her.

Gullible?

One sob sorry, one exquisite night of passionate love-making and she'd been going to throw away the story of a lifetime.

Gullible wasn't the word.

When would she ever learn?

Her call to Trevor was short and to the point. He wanted to know when he would have his story, his pictures.

'His Serene Highness has invited me to join him as his guest at Ascot. On Ladies' Day.'

A formal invitation had arrived in the post that

morning, obviously despatched by his efficient staff before he'd discovered who and what she was. 'His Serene Highness Prince Alexander Orsino requests the pleasure of Miss Laura Varndell'.

He'd already had the pleasure. Now he was going to pay for it.

'I'll deliver my story—' with pictures courtesy of Jay '—the same evening.'

'In time for the first edition,' he warned.

'I guarantee it. I think you'll want to reserve the banner blurb beneath the masthead, space for a front page picture and the whole of page three.'

'Is that right? And who made you editor when I wasn't looking?' She didn't answer him. 'Just what have you got, Laura?'

'An exclusive that will make all your rivals green with envy.'

There was a long, eloquent pause before he said, 'I must be crazy even listening to you.'

'No, Trevor. You're fine.'

She was the crazy one.

She'd have her scoop. This one time she'd prove to everyone that she wasn't a complete fool.

And when she'd done that, she'd look for a job she could live with.

She bought the spare part for her food mixer, then wandered around the kitchen department of Claibournes, her mind on anything but the beautiful cookware as she checked her watch. He was late.

Oddly, she never doubted that he'd come. Maybe she was fooling herself, but last night he hadn't acted like a man totally in control of his emotions. If that was Xander being cynical, she wasn't sure she would survive a night of no holds barred sincerity.

She picked up a cast iron skillet; anything to distract her from thinking about last night. Something was bugging her and it wasn't just the fact that he was late.

Then she looked up and what she saw drove everything else from her mind. Xander was standing on the other side of the display. How long had he been there, watching her? What had he seen?

Her face, she was well aware, wore her feelings like a placard.

She turned away quickly and led the way out through the store, cutting through the food hall to avoid the main entrance and slipping her dark glasses on her nose as she stepped into the street. Grateful that the sunshine gave her the excuse to hide behind them.

'Where are we going?' he asked, falling in beside her, threading his fingers through hers. Startled, she jumped, looked up. He just smiled. 'Relax, I wasn't followed.'

'What?' she demanded guiltily. Then she realised he meant by news photographers. 'Oh, no, of course not.'

'So?'

'Um, right. Today we do urban survival. First stop the Underground.'

'What happened to our bus ride into the country? I had my heart set on a quiet lunch in some riverside inn.'

He did? For a moment she almost succumbed to the temptation to ditch their shadow and make a run for it. Almost. She only had to remind herself what he'd done.

'That's advanced ordinary. First you have to learn the basics.' And she paused at the entrance to the Underground and invited him to step inside.

'Okay,' he said, as he studied the list of destinations. 'Does it matter where we go?'

'It helps to have a destination in mind. That way you have to use the map. What about Regent's Park?' she suggested. 'You'll feel right at home there, I should think.'

That earned her a thoughtful look before he sorted out the fare zone and found sufficient change to purchase two tickets.

'You'd have been better off buying an all-day ticket,' she said when he'd finished, but not with any real enthusiasm. He'd slipped beneath her empathy barrier and she was finding it very hard to evict him. 'They're cheaper and you wouldn't have had to go through that performance again next time.'

'Well, thanks for telling me.'

'The facts were all there. You just had to look.'

'Maybe I'd be better on my own. You're something of a distraction.'

Wordlessly she indicated the barrier, took a ticket from him and demonstrated how it worked. 'I'm not here to hold your hand, Xander. Simply to show you the way.'

He took her hand firmly in his, not letting go even when they reached the escalator. Clearly determined to prove her wrong.

'It's a pity we've missed the rush hour,' she said. 'This is a lot more fun when there are a thousand other people trying to do it at the same time.' Of course, holding hands in such a crush would have been a complete non-starter.

'I'm happy to pass on that delight. So, tell me, what is there to see at Regent's Park?'

See? She'd hadn't given that a thought. Simply been attempting to annoy him a little. If he was irritable with her, she wouldn't feel so damned guilty about doing this...

'Grass?' she offered, as he headed for the nearest platform.

She considered pointing out that they would be going the wrong way, then decided to leave it to him to discover it for himself, the way everyone else did.

'Ordinary grass?' he enquired, with a hint of a smile.

'Of course ordinary grass. And the simple, everyday freedom of a walk in the park.'

Which dealt with the smile.

'There's nothing ordinary or simple about...' He looked as if he'd say more, biting back the words.

'Tunnel out, Xander,' she advised him. 'Abdicate. Declare a republic.'

'You're a subversive, my love. A rebel. A dangerous revolutionary.'

'Of course. My mother was—'

'I know,' he said, laughing. Then, more seriously, 'But I was raised to serve. If I abandoned my responsibilities, my people, what would I do with the rest of my life?'

About to say that that he wouldn't have to do a damn thing, she thought better of it. He'd been raised to serve the people of Montorino and would do so until his dying breath. With or without a title. 'My mistake,' she said. 'I'd apologise, but I know your views on kissing in public.'

The buffeting rush of wind heralding the arrival of a train prevented him from responding. But he looked as if he might have said—or done—a great deal. Instead, he took her arm as they boarded the train and, ignoring the scattered vacant seats, opted to stand by the door so that they could stay close.

She reached for the safety grip, but he beat her to it, looping his arm about her waist, holding her against his chest to keep her from losing her footing as the train started. Keeping her there as it rattled through the tunnels.

It felt so solid. So safe.

Too safe.

As the train drew into the next station, she said, 'Let's go.'

'We have to change?'

'No. You've done the Underground. Let's try a bus next.'

'And this would take us to...?'

'Nowhere,' she said, spotting an open-topped bus. 'Let's catch that and act like a couple of tourists out for the day. We can get on and off wherever we like. We could take out a rowing boat on the Serpentine. Check out the guards at Buckingham Palace before feeding the ducks in St James's.' It would make it easier for Jay to follow them with her battered old Nikon. Who would notice one more tourist taking pictures of the sights? 'Maybe finish the day taking a trip on the London Eye. Look at the city from four hundred and fifty feet up in the air. How does that sound?'

'Ambitious,' he suggested. 'For a girl who's afraid of heights.'

'I'd forgotten,' she said, shocked. The bus moved off without them. 'That's so weird. I just got carried away.'

'I know exactly how that feels, Laura.'

'You do?'

'I had the same thing happen to me just yesterday.' He grasped her hand. 'Come on, let's walk.'

'Well, that was different,' Xander said dryly, as they reached the corner of her street. His eyes crinkled up into a warm smile. 'But fun.'

'Really? Even the Underground?'

'Even the Underground. Although I have to say that had more to do with the company than the surroundings.'

'I'm sorry about the London Eye. I really thought I could do it.'

'I understand. Truly.'

'Even after queuing all that time?'

Laura felt terrible. How could he not see through her? She'd been acting her aching heart out as she'd teased him through a day designed to give him a workout in ordinary life that he'd never forget. Never letting the smile slip for a moment.

At least, she'd been acting until that moment at the London Eye when, on the point of boarding, she'd made the fatal mistake of looking up at the four hundred and fifty-foot ride and had turned into a gibbering wreck.

After that everything had been had been totally real. Just the thought was enough to bring it all flooding back. The blood draining from her face, her legs buckling as she had clutched for the rail… The murmur of impatience building behind them as she had stalled the boarding process.

Her anguished cry for help…

'Xander!'

Even as she began to slip away into the blackness of total panic, he was there, rock-like beside her, his arm about her waist, keeping her on her feet, standing protectively between her and the great wheel towering above her. 'I'm here, sweetheart. You're safe.'

'Don't let me go. Don't ever let me go…'

'Never,' he swore. Then again, 'Never.' And for a moment the terror receded. 'But we're holding everyone up. Come on, let's get away from here.'

'I c-c-can't…' Her mouth continued working, but the words were stuck somewhere inside her head. She couldn't speak. She couldn't move. And, frozen to the spot, she could neither advance nor retreat.

Then, as she began to shake, crumple, he bent and caught her beneath the knees, picked her up and carried her away from the crowd.

She curled against him, burrowing against the solid comfort of his chest, keeping her eyes tight shut. Only opening them when he gently lowered her on to a long wooden settle bench in the quiet corner of a nearby pub. Even then he didn't leave her, but kept his arm tightly around her, holding her close as, with no more than a glance at the barman, he summoned brandy.

He held the glass to her lips. She didn't need spirits

to fortify her. She was drawing all the strength she needed from Xander. But she sipped obediently.

'This is getting to be a habit,' she said, feeling foolish beyond imagining as the panic gradually receded.

Had she really begged him not to let go of her?

Had he really said 'never'?

'Me going wobbly, you plying me with brandy.'

Attempting to make a joke of it.

'Tell me,' he said. Not laughing. And, before she could pretend not to understand, 'About being afraid of heights.'

'It's nothing. Really.' She made an effort to gather herself. Straighten up. Act like a grown-up. 'I can't think what came over me—'

Too late to pull away. He wasn't letting her go.

'Tell me, Laura.' And suddenly she did need the brandy. Took a gulp. 'Your father was a mountaineer. Did he fall to his death? Is that it?'

She shook her head. It was worse, much worse than that. 'He wasn't climbing. That would have been bearable, somehow. If it had been his own mistake…' She swallowed, fighting back tears. It had been a long time since she'd cried. 'If he'd been doing what he loved most…'

Xander waited.

'I'm not afraid of mountains. Only of tall buildings. Tall things…' And she shivered again.

'I'm glad.' She looked at him. 'If you were afraid of mountains then a visit to Montorino would be a painful experience. I hope you will visit?'

For a moment he had succeeded in distracting her totally. When she remained silent, but with surprise rather than fear, he said, 'Tell me, Laura. It helps to get things out in the open. Fear grows in the dark.' He took her hand, held it. 'Trust me, Laura.'

Guilt arrowed through her. She could never go to Montorino, not after today. But she could tell him this truth about herself. Share something that she normally kept locked away, deep inside.

'My parents took a cable car ride. He wasn't climbing. She wasn't writing a travel feature. They were just acting like a couple of tourists for once. Having fun. A helicopter clipped the cable.'

'Cara…' He held her, murmuring soft words of comfort, his lips against her hair. 'I'm so sorry.' He thumbed away tears, kissing her damp cheeks. 'If I'd known—'

'It's not your fault, Xander. It's mine. I don't know how I ever thought I could do that.' Except, somehow, when she was with Xander anything seemed possible. 'I was fine until I looked up and then suddenly everything rushed towards me as if I was falling. Like the nightmares…'

'You still have them?' he asked.

She shivered. 'Not often.'

'Can I help?'

She looked into his eyes—warm, tender. 'You could kiss me better,' she said.

'Now?'

'Now.'

And he lifted her face, kissed her mouth, regardless of the fact that they were in a very public place…

It had been the sweetest kiss. So tender, so giving. But she pushed it from her mind now as he turned to face her, removing the dark glasses she'd clung to in an effort to hide her innermost feelings rather than as a disguise.

'That's better. I've missed your eyes. They show me everything that you feel.' He looked at her for a long time, then gently grazed her temple with his knuckles. 'You're tired, yes?'

'No, I'm fine. Really.'

'I think not. You have been hiding it behind these, determined to keep going for me.'

'Actually, Xander—' she said, unable to bear his kindness any more '—it's the red rims from bawling my eyes out that I've been covering up. I'm sorry I made such a fool of myself.'

'Sweet Laura.' The way he said her name, with a subtly different inflection from the way anyone else had said it ever before, just broke her heart.

'You wanted to talk to me, Xander,' she pressed, in an effort to shatter the intimacy of the moment. She knew what he would say to her, but she needed to hear it now. His warning that, no matter how tender, how sweet, this was just an interlude in his life. Could never be anything more.

While she still owned enough of her heart to salvage something from the inevitable wreckage.

'Maybe over dinner?' he suggested, refusing to be pushed.

'Dinner?'

'Somewhere with a tablecloth and plates and knives and forks,' he prompted.

'Is this a hint that you didn't enjoy our urban picnic at a burger bar?'

'Oh, is that what it was? I did wonder.'

Damn Alexander Orsino. He'd got his role all

wrong. He wasn't supposed to do this teasing stuff, respond with charm and good humour to everything she'd put him through as if he'd been riding the Underground and buses all his life. Feeding the ducks as if it was the most fun he'd ever had.

He was supposed to hate it and be bored and arrogant and—

'Well?' he prompted.

'Well, I don't know,' she said, forcing herself to tease back. 'Will I need a tiara?'

Her face felt as though it would crack from smiling so much when all she wanted to do was bury her head beneath a pillow and weep. Right after she'd got beneath the shower and scrubbed herself clean.

This morning, angry, she had thought it would be easy to do this. But, some time between looking up and seeing him across a pile of cast-iron cookware at Claibournes and lying on the grass in Hyde Park licking at ice cream cones, it had stopped being easy and had become the hardest thing in the world.

She was pretty sure that His Serene Highness Prince Alexander had never, in all his life, been turned down for a date. He would never know how close he came just then. Not because she didn't want to go. In spite of everything, the thought of having dinner with him in some quiet little restaurant where no one knew either of them set her foolish heart playing leap-frog.

Because she wanted it too much.

Fortunately for his ego, if not her peace of mind, she couldn't walk away, job done. With Jay's help she would have the photographs she'd promised Trevor. And she had a story, too. Not the original hatchet job she'd planned, but a story about a prince taking time out in the real world, doing everyday things that would, she knew, fascinate readers worldwide.

But the job wasn't done.

She'd promised Katie three months of anonymity, and for that she had to put herself in the public eye.

And suddenly it all made sense. He was keeping up the pretence, going through with this, for Katie. Then he'd walk away, leaving her to spend the next few months hounded by the press, her every move subjected to long lens scrutiny.

The biter bit. Her just deserts.

She would deliver and gladly. Then maybe she would be able to live with herself.

She took a deep breath. 'Dinner will be lovely, Xander.'

'I will pick you up at eight.' He touched his fingers to her lips as she began to object. 'No,' he said. 'No more cloak and dagger. Today I allowed you to dictate our itinerary. In this age of equality I know you will allow me to do the same this evening.'

He took her phone from his pocket. The screen showed messages waiting.

'I've been keeping you from your life, Laura. The man who wanted to talk to you about a job is getting impatient.'

'It doesn't matter. It's not a job I want. I realise now that I've been looking in entirely the wrong direction.' She managed half a smile, hoping that he would remember that and maybe understand. 'I'll see you later.'

He watched her down the steps to her front door,

for all the world like a lover finding it impossible to tear himself away.

As for her, only the thought that she would see him again in a couple of hours made the separation bearable.

The biter bit, indeed. And the wound was apparently fatal.

CHAPTER NINE

JAY handed Laura a tall glass. 'You look as if you could do with this.'

'How did you guess?' She sipped the gin and tonic. Put it down. Looked at the photographs spread across the dining room table. Touching each of the images. Remembering each moment, captured for ever on film by her brilliant aunt.

Xander's fingers entwined in hers as they'd walked along the street.

The frown creasing his forehead as he'd been confronted with the unfamiliar.

His face, one moment wreathed in laughter, the next all concern as she'd thrown her wobbly as they were about to board the London Eye.

Remembering other moments that had been private. The way he'd held her hands around the brandy glass as he soothed her, reassured her, listened to her pouring out her fears. He'd been so gentle, so tender.

How she would miss that.

Then she saw what must have been the first photograph Jay took. It caught him in the moment before she'd looked up and seen him. There was something so vulnerable in his expression, so heartbreakingly exposed. Almost as if he was hurting as much as she was.

She pushed it away, unable to bear even to look at it.

Then she looked up and saw that Jay was watching her, waiting for her reaction. 'These are brilliant,' she said, the words fighting their way through a throat stuffed with boulders.

'I am pleased with them,' she said. 'It's very gratifying to discover that I haven't lost my touch,' she went on, picking up a photograph of the two of them sitting at an open air café in the park, where they'd stopped for coffee. 'The dark glasses were a nice touch. They give an air of mystery. Who is this anonymous woman in Prince Alexander's life?' She looked up. 'It's impossible to make out what you're thinking. Feeling.'

'That's what makes them so good.'

'When will you give them to Trevor?'

'Trevor?'

'When is he expecting you to deliver them?' Jay pressed.

She gathered up the precious images, the day they represented, and held them against her breast as if to protect them. 'I can't do that,' she whispered, almost to herself. Then she repeated it, louder. 'I can't do it, Jay. Trevor was right all along. You were right—' She looked down at the picture of Xander standing alone, before she'd seen him. A tear splashed on to the glossy image and she wiped it carefully away. 'I can't go through with it.'

'The dark glasses weren't for the photographs, then. They were to hide your feelings from Alexander.'

'I know you'll never understand. You've done so much for me, called in favours every time I messed up, and now, when it's all happened for me, I'm throwing it away…' She'd been going to say, *for love.*

But that was one foolishness she intended to keep to herself.

Then, still clutching them close to her, 'I don't have any right to ask you, Jay. These are your photographs. Your copyright.'

'Oh, please do ask me!' she begged. 'You cannot know how happy I am that you've finally seen the light.'

'What?' She stared at Jay.

'Accepted the truth. If it means you're going to stop beating yourself up trying to be me and your mother, all rolled into one—that you've realised being yourself is enough—then burning these will be worth every penny.'

Laura didn't understand. 'You're not angry with me?'

'Angry? I was beginning to despair. I tossed you the hardest story I could think of, hoping that you would finally realise that you aren't cut out for this, and what happened? You land the story of the year. I was always afraid you would, and then you'd be stuck for ever in a job that would only have made you unhappy.'

Laura sat down rather suddenly. 'But you encouraged me, helped me…'

'It was what you wanted. I would have done anything to make you happy. Maybe, if I'd been your real mother, I wouldn't have been so afraid to say no when you first came to me. Not that you'd have listened…'

She opened her mouth to defend herself. Then

closed it again. Then grinned, quite unbelievably dizzy with relief. 'Of course not.'

'Poor Trevor. If you'd just had that touch of ruthlessness you'd have been so brilliant. He knew it too, that's why he got so angry with you.'

Laura groaned. 'He'll kill me. I told him to hold the front page photo spot, give me the blurb banner, page three—'

'When are you supposed to deliver?'

'The evening of Ladies' Day. I'll have to let him know.' And she'd have to tell Xander, too. The whole truth. She picked up the photographs. Then kissed Jay, hugged her. 'You've been a wonderful mother, Jay. Thank you. For everything.'

'My pleasure. I enjoyed my day trailing after the pair of you, although I bailed out when you walked away from the London Eye. I'd queued too long to miss the ride. Are you seeing Alexander tonight?'

'He's taking me to dinner. In fact, I have to go and get ready. I'll give him these, Jay. Tell him everything.'

'You're sure?'

'Absolutely sure.'

'What about Ascot?'

'I promised. That's for Katie, so I know he'll do it.'

'Then I'll treat you to something special to wear. And leave Trevor to me. I'll break it to him gently that his scoop got away. I don't suppose he'll be completely surprised.'

She wore black. Simple, elegant and somehow appropriate. Put up her hair. Long jet drops in her ears.

Fastened a black velvet band around her throat to which she'd pinned the gold Montorino coat of arms that he'd given her.

She wanted to wear it, just once.

Then, when she was ready, she sat and wrote a letter to Xander, telling him everything, the whole story, before putting it with the photographs and wrapping them all in gold paper. They were, after all, worth a fortune.

The clock was striking eight as she tied the slender package with ribbon, and as the last chime died away there was an echoing ring at the doorbell. Arranging her features into the nearest approximation of a smile she could manage, she went to open it. And the smile froze on her face.

It wasn't Xander. It was the footman.

'Miss Varndell,' he said, with the slightest bow. 'His Highness asked me to give you this.'

It was a square envelope made from the kind of paper that would last a thousand years. She took it, said, 'Thank you.'

What else could she say?

Apparently the man assumed he was being dismissed because he said, 'I am to wait.'

She shrugged, prised back the flap and took out the single sheet of paper and opened it up.

My apologies, Laura. I cannot get away but Phillip will bring you to me. I'll explain when I see you. Xander.

Any doubt about her feelings for him would have been dispelled by her reaction to that note. The rush of relief, of joy.

She picked up her wrap, her evening purse, the slender gold package, and followed Phillip to the gleaming Rolls parked at the kerb. Nothing low-key about that.

Phillip opened the door for her and bowed slightly as she climbed in, before joining the chauffeur in the front passenger seat. Leaving her to ride in state in the rear.

As the busy evening traffic melted before them she allowed herself a moment of fantasy. How would it be to live like this? Before she could decide whether it would be wonderful or horrible, they had swept into the mews behind Xander's residence from where Phillip led her, in some state, through to the vast entrance hall and then bowed. 'His Highness is in his study. He requested that you go straight up.'

'Thank you.' Then, because she couldn't think what else to say, 'Nice ride.'

'I find the flag always does the trick, ma'am,' he said.

Flag? She'd ridden through London in a car flying a royal standard? Was that legal?

'Er, right,' she said. 'I'll, um, have to try that on my bike.'

And, amazingly, Mr Snooty grinned. 'I'll see if we have a spare, ma'am.'

Then she turned and took the stairs two at a time. Whatever was happening, she wanted it over with. Now. She burst into Xander's study. 'You didn't have to go through all that drama, you know,' she said, not giving him a chance to speak first. 'If you wanted me here, you could have just phoned. I'd have got a cab—' Her voice dried in her throat as she saw his face, so different from when he'd said goodbye just a few hours earlier. Recognised the lines of anxiety etched into it. 'What's happened?'

'Katie is missing.'

She abandoned the things she was carrying on the nearest sofa and crossed to him, took his hands, all other thoughts driven from her head. 'When? How? Did she arrive home safely?'

'Her mother rang at lunchtime. She was almost incoherent with worry when I spoke to her. It would seem that she took off almost as soon as she got home.'

'She's been missing all night? Why didn't Karl page you?'

'Because I left the pager behind. I didn't want anything to disturb our day.'

She felt the colour leave her face. She'd been playing follow my leader with him around London and all the while he'd been needed here. 'Xander, I'm so sorry.'

'No,' he said quickly. 'Please don't say that.'

'You want to keep all the guilt for yourself, huh?' He stared at her. She shook her head, this was not the moment to indulge herself with guilty confessions. 'Tell me what happened.'

'The plane arrived on time. She was met, driven home. She apparently told my sister that she felt unwell after the flight and went straight to bed. Charlotte had to go to some charitable function and left her to it.'

'And then?' she pressed.

He dragged his hand over his face. 'Her maid went up at about eight o'clock to see if she wanted anything but when she saw Katie was still asleep she didn't disturb her. She knew she'd get herself something from the kitchen if she was hungry later.'

'Should I be impressed at this evidence of self-sufficiency?'

He managed a brief smile. 'Not very,' he admitted. Then, 'My sister didn't get up until lunchtime, at which point she finally decided it was time she had a heart-to-heart with her tiresome daughter. That's when she discovered that the mound beneath the covers was not in fact Katie, but some artfully arranged pillows.'

'No one had missed her by lunchtime?'

'She usually gets her own breakfast when she's home and then goes out riding. But for Charlotte's unaccustomed attack of maternal duty, no one would have missed her until evening.'

'She's turning into quite an escape artist, isn't she? Obviously the subterfuge was to gain time.'

'You warned me.'

'So I did, but really you shouldn't blame yourself.'

'Why not? Who else is there?'

'Xander, she has a mother, and presumably somewhere a father.'

'Not one that distinguishes himself with his presence. He was one of my sister's more impressive mistakes. Or do I mean less impressive?' He made a helpless gesture and let it go. 'If I hadn't made such a point of ramming home my message, if I'd treated her like an adult and let her into my confidence—'

Laura couldn't bear to see him in such distress and she put her arms around him.

'Shh,' she said, holding him.

He clung to her for a moment, as if to a life raft. 'She could be anywhere, Laura.'

'No, no. She hasn't just run off into the night.' In fact, she had a pretty good idea exactly where she'd run to. Or at least who. 'She had plenty of time to plan this. From the moment she left my flat.' She considered sharing her belief that Katie had called the photographer herself, to get herself some breathing space. Decided against it.

'That is supposed to make me feel better? What do they say about the road to hell being paved with good intentions?'

She leaned back, looked up at him. 'Hey, come on. Look on the bright side.'

'Bright side?' he demanded, with disbelief. 'And that is?'

'Well, for one thing, this time I don't think she's been kidnapped.'

He brushed that aside as nonsense. 'Please tell me that there's a second thing.'

'For two—' she said '—you won't have to pay for her fare back to London.'

'You think I care—?'

'Xander,' she said, cutting him short. 'Put yourself in her shoes. You're young, in love and you're really, really angry with someone in authority. Where would you go for comfort, succour? And to seriously tick off the grown-ups?'

The answer to the first part was easy, Xander thought, holding Laura close. He'd been angry, absolutely livid with Katie, with his sister, with himself. Angry and more frightened than he could ever remember. It was a moment to batten down the hatches, keep a lid on this, lock out everyone but close family, trusted advisers. And the only person he had wanted to be with him was Laura. Against every principle by which he governed his life, he had turned to her.

An outsider.

He'd brought her here and he had been right.

She had cut through all the nonsense, the headless chicken act of his sister, the grim prognostications of everyone else, his own sickening sense of guilt.

'If you're suggesting that she flew straight back to London, you're wrong. I've already checked that. She didn't catch any flight that left Montorino in the last twenty-four hours.'

'Men are so obvious,' she said. 'They think in straight lines. Whereas teenage girls are devious little minxes. She wouldn't go straight back to the airport in Montorino where everyone knew her. Where they might ask awkward questions. But Europe has open borders. She could have crossed into Italy in a couple of hours and flown from there. All it would have taken would have been one phone call to a friend. Speaking of which…'

She wriggled from his arms and, reaching for her bag, took out her tiny cellphone.

'Have you got the number of her cellphone?' she asked.

'You're going to try calling her? Don't you think I've tried that? And her mother? We've both left messages.'

'Saying what? Come home, you bad girl? And be

locked up until adolescence is safely over?' She reached out, touched his hand in a gesture of comfort. 'She doesn't want to go home, my love. And she's certainly not going to call back just to get yelled at.'

'I didn't—I wouldn't!' He raised his hands in surrender. 'You seem to have a pretty fair grasp of the situation, although why you think she will listen to you—'

'It's worth a try. I think she trusts me.'

She looked up at him then, momentarily uncertain, almost, he thought, as if he might query that.

'Of course she trusts you. You stood up for her, took her part, fought for her right to some freedom.'

'I meant it, Xander.'

'I know, I was listening. Just not quite hard enough.'

And he told her the number and waited while she listened to it ring.

'I'm getting the voicemail prompt,' she said. Then, 'Katie, I go out of my way to plead your cause with some success I might add—and you do this to me.'

She shifted the phone to her other ear as she paced the carpet.

'I am so cross with you. Okay, Xander didn't handle the situation very well—' she held up a finger to stop him from interrupting '—but his heart is in the right place. All by himself he'd decided to fly you, economy class so you wouldn't attract attention, back to London at the weekend. He arranged for you to stay with some old nanny while you're at school over here. Pretty much total freedom. All you had to do was keep your head down and avoid doing anything stupid. Like getting arrested for being in a nightclub when you're under age,' she added, presumably to remind the wretched girl what had caused all the fuss in the first place. 'Or running away.' Then, 'I think I can persuade him to stick to that plan...'

She looked at him for confirmation and he nodded. He'd have done anything.

'He's nodding, okay? But forget Xander for a moment. I'm laying down some conditions here. First, you phone your mother and get her off your uncle's back before she completely messes up our evening. Second, you get yourself over to this nanny person right now.' She paused. 'There was something else.' She looked at him. 'Oh, right, I remember. Give Michael a kiss from me.'

She cut the connection. 'Now we wait.'

'How long?'

'Well, the phone will bleep to tell her there's a message. Whether she takes any notice rather depends on how guilty she's feeling. And what else she has to occupy her.'

'Please, I don't want to think about what else she might be doing. Long enough,' he enquired, 'for me to show you how much I appreciate your help? Far from ordinary clear thinking. Ability to handle tiresome teenagers...'

'There isn't enough time in the world—'

'I'm making time,' he said, and was still kissing her when his relieved sister rang five minutes later to let them know the crisis was over.

'So,' he said, replacing the receiver. 'Let's get out of here.'

'You're not going to wait for Katie to ring you?'

'I am not going to waste another moment of this

evening worrying about my niece.' He took her mobile phone and switched it off before putting it in his pocket. 'And neither are you. Did I mention that you look absolutely stunning?'

'No.' Laura lifted her brows encouragingly. She was only human.

He took both her hands in his, lifted them, kissed them. 'You look absolutely stunning. Interesting brooch. There's a matching set.'

'You can have too much of a good thing,' she assured him.

'Impossible.' For a moment he held her with his eyes, as if he was thinking of something other than gold. Then he crossed swiftly to the telephone and rapped out an order. 'One moment more.'

The doors opened and Phillip appeared with a small stool which he placed in front of Laura. He was followed by an elderly man carrying a large leather-covered box.

'Laura,' Xander said, indicating the stool.

'No, Xander. Absolutely not.'

'Can you not forget for a moment that you're a republican with a small R and indulge the Crown Prince of Montorino?'

'Not in this instance.'

'Very well. Karl—' He snapped his fingers and the older man stepped forward with the box, opened it, and Xander lifted the vivid blue bow of the Order ribbon before waving the two men from the room in a demonstration of imperiousness that left Laura gaping. Then, when they'd gone, he grinned. 'I have a reputation to keep up,' he said. 'And you are doing it no good whatsoever.' Then he pinned the bow, with its enamel miniature of his grandfather, to her shoulder. 'For services to the State of Montorino, I invest you with the Order of Merit, first class.'

'First class?' she asked, biting back a ridiculous mixture of laughter and tears.

'You deserve nothing less.'

She touched it with her fingers. 'I'll treasure it, Your Highness.' Then, 'I have something for you, too.' She looked around for the package and gave it to him before she lost her nerve. As he reached for the bow she said, 'You mustn't open it until you're on your own.'

'Is that a gentle hint that last night was a one-off?' he asked, then looked up, straight into her eyes, with an intensity that almost took her breath away.

'Last night was very special, Xander. But it was out of character, for me as well as for you.' She held his gaze. 'That *was* what you wanted to say to me? This morning? This afternoon? It's all right, my love. We both know that this isn't a lifetime commitment. You don't do that.'

'Actually, that wasn't what I was going to say, but don't worry about it. It will wait until we've eaten. I'm absolutely famished.'

And he slipped the package into his pocket, took her arm and led her down the huge curving staircase and out of the front entrance to the waiting Rolls.

CHAPTER TEN

THE restaurant Xander had chosen was by the river. The food was heavenly, the atmosphere impressively romantic. Very far from ordinary.

'This is cheating, you know. We should be having pasta at some cheerful trattoria with a bottle of Chianti.'

'I know, but I wanted—' He stopped. 'Oh, look, this is no good. I keep putting it off, but I have to get it over with.' He pushed away the fine pâté he'd been toying with and summoned the waiter. 'Will you please ask the chef to hold the next course?' The man paled. Xander, however, was already on his feet. 'Will you walk with me, Laura? I can't put this off any longer.'

Oh, great.

As if one of them feeling guilty wasn't bad enough.

He led her out on to the small dock, slipping off his jacket and putting it around her shoulders when she shivered. Actually it wasn't cold but apprehension that goosed her flesh, but the jacket was warm from his body and deeply comforting for that alone.

'I have to confess that I did something dreadful yesterday,' he said. 'That's what I've been trying to say to you all day.'

'Dreadful?' Her voice squeaked.

'Yesterday afternoon, when you fell asleep in the garden.'

She felt sick. He was going to tell her that he knew that she was a journalist and then she was going to have to tell him the whole truth, make him look at the photographs. And then he would put her in a taxi, if she was lucky, and send her home.

End of story. End of everything.

'You looked around my flat?' she asked jokingly to forestall him. 'To make sure I wasn't some foreign spy?' His startled reaction would have been funny. If her heart hadn't been breaking.

'You knew.'

She shrugged as if it didn't matter. 'Just as long as you didn't go through my underwear drawer I can forgive you.'

'Can you? And if it was worse than that?'

'Worse than the underwear drawer?' she asked, wanting him to laugh, do anything but say the words, *Is there anything worse?*

His expression suggested anything but humour. 'I could pretend to you that I had a sudden attack of cautiousness. That I'd realised just how far out on a limb I'd crawled. That I was simply protecting myself from the possibility that you weren't just a lively, lovely girl who I wanted to spend some time with. A lot of time with. Quite probably the rest of my life with.'

Her heart missed a beat. And then another one. She thought it might never beat again.

'Actually, I did pretend that. To myself. Told myself that you could be anyone. That I had left myself wide open. It was uncharacteristic of me.'

'But?' she asked, suddenly wanting to hear everything.

'The truth? I was just…jealous. I heard you on the phone, laughing. And I was jealous. So when you were asleep I plugged in your phone and used the redial button to find out who you had called.'

Jealous? He really had been jealous? She didn't know whether to laugh or cry. Tears seemed more likely.

'And?' He was staring at the water, his confession apparently over. 'That's all you did?'

He glanced up at her. 'I betrayed your trust. Isn't it enough?' He straightened, then shrugged. 'Of course you're right to be suspicious. Natural caution, common sense told me to do more. I had my hand on your bag. After all, I was supposed to be protecting my interests. My heart, however, would not allow it.'

He had been honest. She could be no less.

'Your heart let you down, Xander.' As hearts were wont to do at the most inconvenient moments. 'I'm a journalist. I was a journalist. I got the sack the day before I met you. For incompetence,' she added, when his expression silently asked the question. 'I would have done anything to get my job back. I thought I would have done anything.' She took the packet of photographs out of his jacket pocket and gave them to him. 'Actually, I did. I knew you'd checked my redial. My aunt has one of those phones that shows the number of the person calling. She came down this morning to ask me why I'd phoned her and then hung up without speaking. It could only have been you.'

'I see. And this?' he asked, looking at the package as if it might bite.

'This was my revenge. Having checked my phone,

I assumed you'd gone the whole nine yards. If you'd been in my handbag you'd have found the hidden camera and—'

The look on his face stopped her dead.

Keep going. You can do this. 'I thought you must have spoiled the film, so today I had Jay follow us. She was a photojournalist, you see. Those are all the pictures she took.'

He stared at the package in his hand for a moment. Then looked up at her. 'You did this because you thought that last night, when you begged me to love you, when I was lost to all reason with longing, desire, everything that a man can feel for a woman...when I would have given anything to be able to walk away from you and save myself the pain of leaving you... You thought that at that moment I was merely taking cynical advantage of you?'

'Not then. Then I believed—' She lifted her face, shivered as the cool breeze off the river chilled her damp cheeks. 'I'm glad I was wrong. Not that it mattered in the end. Because I couldn't go through with it. Those are the photographs, negatives. I wrote you a note. I tried to explain...'

He touched her cheeks, wiped them with his fingers, drying tears that she hadn't been aware of shedding.

'My heart didn't let me down, Laura. It was my head that did that. Too much logic. But last night, my darling, I confronted reality. I told you I would walk away from any woman I loved enough to share my life with. Because I would spare her that. And I discovered that what was easy to say when you've never been in love is an altogether different matter when you cannot imagine life without that woman.'

Just as well she wasn't princess material. That she was just an ordinary girl. One who was in touch with reality. '"In love" is a temporary madness, Xander. You'll get over it. We both will.'

Maybe.

'A temporary madness, maybe, but one for which you would give away photographs that would earn you a small fortune.'

'Probably,' she admitted.

He smiled then. 'You have already given them. Are they very good photographs?'

She took them from him, opened the package. Handed them to him one at a time. He looked at each one for a long time. 'Your aunt is very talented, Laura. They are beautiful photographs. Bad photographs would have earned you a small fortune. For these you could name your price.'

All that was left in her hand was the note, and she offered it to him. He shook his head. 'I don't need that,' he said. 'There is nothing that I don't already know about you.'

'No.' Well, the word 'journalist' said it all. 'Will you take me home now, please?'

'You think my decision not to marry is an overreaction, don't you?' he said, ignoring her plea.

'It's your choice. I respect it.'

'But you don't understand it. No one does. Only my grandfather.' He put the photographs into his pocket and took her arm, began to walk. 'You're a journalist, so I imagine you've done your homework on the Orsino family. You'll know the official version of how my parents died.'

'In a tragic boating accident. They were out on a lake, a romantic break, a reconciliation after problems with their marriage. There was an explosion, probably a gas leak.'

'It wasn't like that, Laura. My father had been photographed at a party behaving somewhat indiscreetly with another woman. It wasn't spectacularly bad behaviour.' He shrugged. 'Not spectacularly good, either. I'm not making excuses for him but he paid a high price for a moment of stupidity. But you know how it is—when you're heir to an ancient throne everything you do is interesting to a certain section of the press. Especially the stupid things.'

'I don't understand. What has this to do with the explosion?'

'My mother was fragile. There were, as you've heard, rumours that their marriage was in trouble. The truth was that she'd had a series of miscarriages and was suffering from severe depression. She already felt a complete failure as a wife, a woman, and when she saw that photograph she wrote my father a note, begging his forgiveness for letting him down so badly. Then she took an overdose. When my father found her, read the note, he shot himself. The reconciliation—the boating accident—the explosion—it was all a stage-managed cover-up by my grandfather to explain the two deaths and the fact that my father's coffin had to be closed.'

'He told you this?' she asked, horrified.

'No, it was my grandmother. When she was dying. I was getting something of a reputation myself and she was afraid I was going to repeat my father's mistakes. She wanted to warn me how easy it is to hurt someone beyond repair.'

That was when he'd sought the sanctuary of Juliet's family home. Decided to change his life. And even that had been disturbed by press intrusion. No wonder he hated them all so much, she thought. She reached out, took his hand, held it.

'I'm so sorry.'

He turned to her. 'I didn't tell you so that you would feel sorry for me, Laura. I told you because I wanted to show you that I trust you. I am now entirely in your hands. My entire family is now in your hands.' He took them, held them palm up. 'Right here.'

'You are safe enough, Xander. I set out to find the man behind the prince,' she said. 'I found him.'

'You did more than that. You changed him. I don't know how else to show my sincerity. My total faith in you.'

'It is not misplaced. Truly. I will hold your secrets in my heart.'

'And me? Is there room in your heart for an unreconstructed, arrogant autocrat?'

'Xander?'

'I am asking if there is any way that a republican—one with a very small R—could ever consider becoming a princess?'

She could scarcely breathe. 'So what happened to the "love a woman enough to walk away" scenario?'

'I was twenty-three when I made that decision. Young. Hurting. Afraid that my grandmother was right. And between then and now I have not met a woman with the strength to jerk me out of that self-pity.'

'No!'

'I met you, desired you from the moment I first set eyes on you. And then I fell in love with you. Nothing else would have brought me to your flat, carrying your jacket like my own footman.'

'Oh.'

'You begged me to love you, Laura. I was a long way ahead of you. And now I find that despite the noble gestures, fine words, walking away is not an option. You are strong, Laura. Together we will be unbeatable. Will you marry me? Be my wife.'

'But... But...' This was ridiculous. 'I can't marry you.'

'I'm afraid you must, cara.... How else can I be sure my secrets are safe?'

On the point of declaring vehemently that she would never betray him, she stopped. 'Well, yes,' she said seriously. 'I suppose that would be a constant worry for you.'

'The only alternative is to have you locked up in the Tower.'

'For the tourists to gawp at?'

He finally smiled. 'I'd come every day.'

'Xander, it's impossible. I'm far too *ordinary*.'

'The world needs more ordinary princesses, my love. With heart, compassion, honour. Will you be my princess, my darling? Use your wonderful spirit and charm to help me take my country into this new century?' He raised her palms to his lips, then looked up directly into her eyes. 'I know you'll forgive me for mentioning this, but you are going to need a new career.'

'Marriage—' she declared roundly '—is not a career.'

'It is when you're sleeping with the head of state.'

'But—' At that point His Serene Highness Prince Alexander Michael George Orsino remembered that he was supposed to be an autocrat. And he decided to act like one.

And the last coherent thought Laura had, for a very long time, was that Trevor would get his exclusive after all.

Their engagement was announced the morning of Ladies' Day at Royal Ascot. Laura drove along the course in an open carriage as part of the royal procession, with Xander beside her and his delighted grandfather and Katie sitting opposite them. The young Princess had declared that she wouldn't miss it for anything—even if it did mean she looked like a pink mushroom.

The following morning it was that photograph which appeared on the front page of every newspaper. But only Trevor had more than the simple details set out in the press release. Only he had a picture feature showing how the Crown Prince of Montorino had courted his ordinary princess. Walking in the park, feeding ducks, and even one of His Serene Highness apparently purchasing an onion at a street market.

The world was charmed, as he had been, by his ordinary princess and their fairy tale romance. And the fees raised by the pictures, syndicated throughout the world, were put into a charitable trust to be administered by Her Serene Highness Princess Laura. Just one of the many important and exciting new jobs awaiting her when she returned from her honeymoon.

But first there was the wedding.

The ceremony took place in September, when there were autumn crocuses in the alpine meadows and the first snows were frosting the highest peaks of the mountains.

Laura arrived at the door of Montorino's ancient cathedral in a fairy tale coach drawn by six white horses. She had no close male relative she wanted to ask to give her away. Jay rode with her, walked with her down the long aisle towards her prince, followed by Katie and half a dozen tiny bridesmaids.

And in that moment she did not feel ordinary. It was nothing to do with the heavy silk of her classically simple gown, its tiny cut-away bolero covering her shoulders and arms in the cathedral. Or the fabulously long train. Or the diamonds in the tiara that Xander had commissioned for her to wear on this day.

It was the look in his eyes as he broke with tradition, left his supporters and walked down the aisle to meet her. The way he held out his hand, as if he was offering her his heart. As she reached for it, took it, held it, it was for a moment as if they were quite alone.

And then he turned and they walked together towards the altar where they would say the vows that would bind them together for ever.

After the grandeur of the wedding they disappeared from the face of the earth for six weeks, lost to the world as they enjoyed the quiet simplicity of Xander's vineyard. Enjoying the harvest festival after the pressing of the grapes.

'Tomorrow we have to stop playing at being rustics and return to normality, my love,' Xander said as he joined her in bed. 'Are you ready for that?'

'Well, I haven't had a lifetime's training like your sister, or Katie,' she said. 'Maybe they could help?'

'Forget I asked. You'll be great. Actually, you're already great. You've done more to raise the profile of Montorino that I could have done in twenty years.'

'I'm glad you appreciate me, because there is something I need to make clear before we go back to the capital. About the future.'

Xander traced a finger down her cheek. 'I'm beginning to recognise that tone in your voice. It's your "you'd better listen to me" voice. The one you used on Katie. And on me when you refused to kneel so that I could invest you with the Order of Merit.'

'I'm glad you realise that.' His fingertip had reached a particularly sensitive spot just below her jaw, and Laura was having a hard time keeping her face straight, her voice firm. 'It means I will only have to say this once.' She caught his hand, held it. 'On the subject of children—'

'Our children?' he murmured, resorting to kissing her shoulder.

'Of course our children.' He stilled. Looked up. 'When they arrive,' she said quickly.

'Tell me about our children arriving,' he said, reclaiming his hand, laying it over her belly.

'Well, the first may be a girl—'

'If it's not a boy,' he agreed.

'And if it's a girl, I will expect her to be treated equally.' *Now* she had his attention. 'In everything.'

'Laura, darling, you cannot fly in the face of a thousand years of history.'

'I can't. I realise that. But you're an autocrat. You can do whatever you want.'

'Is that so? And this being an autocrat—remind me—does it mean that everyone does what I say? Without question?'

'Everyone,' she assured him. 'Except me. We have equal billing in this relationship.'

'We do?' He grinned. 'We do.'

'So I think a decree would do it, something simple. Before the first one arrives would be best.'

His palm stroked the soft curves of her body. 'And are we working to a fixed time frame?'

'Well, there's nothing set in stone, but I thought we might make a start any time in the next few minutes…'

His Serene Highness Prince Alexander Michael George Orsino looked up into the face of his beloved wife and tradition didn't stand a chance.

'Where are you going?' she demanded, as he made a move.

'To draft that decree.'

But she slid down the bed, holding him captive. 'I've already prepared a draft, my prince. You can execute it tomorrow. I've got other plans for tonight.'

Your opinion is important to us! Please take a few moments to share your thoughts with us about your experiences with Harlequin and Silhouette books. Your comments will be very useful in ensuring that we deliver books you love to read.

Please take a few minutes to complete the questionnaire, then send it to us at the address below.

Send your completed questionnaires to:
Harlequin/Silhouette Reader Survey, P.O. Box 9046, Buffalo, NY 14269-9046

1. As you may know, there are many different lines under the Harlequin and Silhouette brands. Each of the lines is listed below. Please check the box that most represents your reading habit for each line.

Line	Currently [illegible] line	Do not [illegible] line	Not sure if [illegible] line
Harlequin American Romance	❑	❑	❑
Harlequin Duets	❑	❑	❑
Harlequin Romance	❑	❑	❑
Harlequin Historicals	❑	❑	❑
Harlequin Superromance	❑	❑	❑
Harlequin Intrigue	❑	❑	❑
Harlequin Presents	❑	❑	❑
Harlequin Temptation	❑	❑	❑
Harlequin Blaze	❑	❑	❑
Silhouette Special Edition	❑	❑	❑
Silhouette Romance	❑	❑	❑
Silhouette Intimate Moments	❑	❑	❑
Silhouette Desire	❑	❑	❑

2. Which of the following best describes why you bought *this book?* One answer only, please.

the picture on the cover	❑	the title	❑
the author	❑	the line is one I read often	❑
part of a miniseries	❑	saw an ad in another book	❑
saw an ad in a magazine/newsletter	❑	a friend told me about it	❑
I borrowed/was given this book	❑	other: ________________	❑

3. Where did you buy *this book?* One answer only, please.

at Barnes & Noble	❑	at a grocery store	❑
at Waldenbooks	❑	at a drugstore	❑
at Borders	❑	on eHarlequin.com Web site	❑
at another bookstore	❑	from another Web site	❑
at Wal-Mart	❑	Harlequin/Silhouette Reader Service/through the mail	❑
at Target	❑	used books from anywhere	❑
at Kmart	❑	I borrowed/was given this book	❑
at another department store or mass merchandiser	❑		

4. On average, how many Harlequin and Silhouette books do you buy at one time?

I buy _______ books at one time ❑
I rarely buy a book ❑

MRQ403HR-1A

5. How many times per month do you shop for any *Harlequin and/or Silhouette* books? One answer only, please.

1 or more times a week	❑	a few times per year	❑
1 to 3 times per month	❑	less often than once a year	❑
1 to 2 times every 3 months	❑	never	❑

6. When you think of your ideal heroine, which *one* statement describes her the best? One answer only, please.

She's a woman who is strong-willed	❑	She's a desirable woman	❑
She's a woman who is needed by others	❑	She's a powerful woman	❑
She's a woman who is taken care of	❑	She's a passionate woman	❑
She's an adventurous woman	❑	She's a sensitive woman	❑

7. The following statements describe types or genres of books that you may be interested in reading. Pick *up to 2 types* of books that you are most interested in.

I like to read about truly romantic relationships	❑
I like to read stories that are sexy romances	❑
I like to read romantic comedies	❑
I like to read a romantic mystery/suspense	❑
I like to read about romantic adventures	❑
I like to read romance stories that involve family	❑
I like to read about a romance in times or places that I have never seen	❑
Other: ________________________________	❑

The following questions help us to group your answers with those readers who are similar to you. Your answers will remain confidential.

8. Please record your year of birth below.

19 ____

9. What is your marital status?

single ❑ married ❑ common-law ❑ widowed ❑
divorced/separated ❑

10. Do you have children 18 years of age or younger currently living at home?

yes ❑ no ❑

11. Which of the following best describes your employment status?

employed full-time or part-time ❑ homemaker ❑ student ❑
retired ❑ unemployed ❑

12. Do you have access to the Internet from either home or work?

yes ❑ no ❑

13. Have you ever visited eHarlequin.com?

yes ❑ no ❑

14. What state do you live in?

____

15. Are you a member of Harlequin/Silhouette Reader Service?

yes ❑ Account # ____________ no ❑ MRQ403HR-1B